Chris Coley was born in Birmingham. After studying Art he worked as a graphic designer before joining the teaching profession in 1994 eventually becoming the Headteacher of a secondary school.

He was inspired to write his first novel, Amber Wolfe and the Shifters, by the courage and determination of his own profoundly deaf daughter.

DEAD HEAD

CHRIS F COLEY

JUMPING FISH

Jumping Fish
An imprint of Peak Platform
Hassop Station
Bakewell
Derbyshire
DE45 1NW

First published by Jumping Fish 2009

Printed in England

A CIP catalogue record for this book is available from the
British Library

ISBN: 978-1-907219- 07-8
www.peakplatform.com

Dedication

To all the many excellent, talented and hard working teachers I have had the pleasure to work with during my time in education.

Acknowledgements

Many thanks to Nessa for acting as my artistic
conscience throughout the production
of this work.
Also, a very special thanks goes to the publisher
for taking the plunge.

FOREWORD

I first met Bob Pike many years ago whilst we were both studying at college. In those days we were two young men training to be teachers and setting out on what we expected to be long careers. Even then, we both harboured dreams of becoming Headteachers.

Bob was always good company; a happy go lucky, fun loving individual with a massive zest for life and a drive and determination to succeed in any activity he participated.

On the rugby field he was an utterly ruthless beast and never went into any conflict without giving an impressive account of himself. Many a strong man left the opposition changing room carrying the scars supplied by Bob "The Killer" Pike.

During one drunken Friday evening session, having wasted oodles of our combined student grant on countless pints of strong ale, we wagered who would be the first to achieve Headship of a school. For many years after this remained a topic of conversation every time we met. We would talk about our latest promotion and our plans to get over the next hurdle in our race for the "big prize." I can still remember the conversation when we made the wager...

'You'll probably win,' said Bob, after we had agreed the terms of our bet, 'you always were a lucky bastard.'

'Then why do you want to take the bet on?' I asked him.

'You know me, never give in, and never admit defeat. Besides I've always got hope on my side.'

Our careers mirrored each other almost perfectly; we were even married in the same year and acted as the Best Man at the other's wedding. We stayed in touch for a long time, but promotions soon cut down the time we had to socialise and eventually we just grew apart. We did send each other the odd Christmas card for a few years and then even this token gesture of friendship stopped.

Some time ago I heard it on the grapevine that he and Val, his wife, had moved much further north when he secured a position in a tough inner city school; for his sake I hope it turned out to be a good move.

Five years ago I fulfilled my ambition and became Headteacher of my own school. Did Bob achieve his wish? I can only hope he did. What kind of Headteacher would he turn out to be? Over the years people change, but the Bob Pike I knew would certainly make an interesting choice as Headteacher. Would he be a good Headteacher to work for? Well he would certainly have support and loyalty from staff, as he always had the uncanny knack of getting on with people.

Would I like to work with him? No, most certainly not.

C.F. Coley, 2009

CHAPTER 1

SHATTERED DREAMS AND PINK PANTIES

"Happiness is like those palaces in fairy tales whose gates
are guarded by dragons: we must fight in
order to conquer it."
Alexandre Dumas

Monday morning and I'm here again. Oh God, how I hate school assemblies. What is the point of rising to the dizzy height of headship only to spend every morning spouting the same sanctimonious twaddle to a bunch of disinterested acne ridden adolescents? If I had wanted to work with children, I would have become a social worker or a scout leader or even, heaven forbid, stayed in the classroom as a bog-standard teacher, but I wanted more than that. I wanted an office of my own, my own extension number, and a personal assistant. I wanted power. I wanted total control.

A few months ago my dream came true when the Headteacher, Mr Ted Shilling, a keen water sport aficionado and fitness freak, suddenly died of heart failure whilst competing in some lame-brained triathlon event.

Consequently, as the senior Deputy, I stepped up in to the role to "keep a firm hand on the tiller" as the Governors put it, until they decided to advertise for a permanent replacement.

As you will appreciate, I have significantly more important things to do than stand on this stage for twenty minutes watching Kieran Roth of 9N scratch his nether regions. Neither do I wish to witness Anthony Guilhoolie, 10M, prise free the contents of his left nostril and proudly display his trophy to his less than ladylike girlfriend, Kelly Watts, self-appointed ringleader and alpha-female of the legendary 10L.

'It's important to understand how vital it is for us to be good citizens; to show we are all prepared to assist each other and lend a helping hand in the same way as the Good Samaritan.'

Not one of them is listening to me. Six hundred faces pointing in my direction, over a thousand unseeing eyes peering out from bodies stuffed with Playstation, junk food, iPhone technology and overactive hormones, why do I bother?

'So please remember to help someone in need if the chance arises. Thank you. Staff, any notices, no? Good, dismissed.'

I leave the crowd control to the minions while I make a hasty exit, stage left, to get back to the important stuff. I successfully negotiate the stampede to lesson one and manage to avoid interacting with a single pupil or member of staff; a skill for which I found I have a natural talent. When I eventually make it back to my office, my personal assistant, Linda Hewlett, (a rather dreary looking woman with an overactive thyroid), is waiting to greet me outside the door to my inner sanctum.

'Yes Linda. What is it?'

'The Chair of Governors is in your office Mr. Pike.'

The Chair of Governors is sometimes the bane of a Headteacher's life and yet, if well managed, can be a positive asset and an ally, especially when you require a pay rise. These creatures are, on the whole, a strange and rare breed. They originate from diverse backgrounds and yet they have one trait in common; they are all immersed in their own sense of self-importance. By day, they may lead simple, humdrum and conventional lives, but place them in the Chair of a Governors' meeting and suddenly they believe they are a management consultant par-excellence, a financial wizard to rival the best brains on Wall Street and a veritable Doctor Bernardo when it comes to the welfare of the youth of society. They are delusional in virtually every case and have no idea just how superficial their jumped up little role is. It is the Head that runs the school, the Head that makes the decisions. Therefore, it is the Head who should be regarded as numero-uno and the Chair of Governors can be of best use by keeping their stuck-up, interfering noses out of school affairs and doing what they're told when required.

'Dorothy is here? How wonderful. Can you arrange coffee for two and a plate of biscuits please, Linda,' I say, even though I know she feels it's beneath the dignity of a Head's PA to organise refreshments for visitors. Still, who is it giving the orders round here?

Dorothy Biggar is sitting down when I enter my office. I hope she's not been snooping over my desk; my diary has several caricatures of her scribbled on the inside cover (what else can I do to occupy myself in a bloody boring Governors meeting?) She's a squat, severe looking woman with thick ankles and gives the impression she has never thought to trouble Aphrodite for an odd favour or two.

'Dorothy, how fantastic to see you,' I lie. 'You're looking as radiant as usual; are you here on business or pleasure?' I ask, knowing full well the old witch only ever comes to school if there has been a complaint or she wants me to do some favour for an acquaintance of hers.

'I've come to talk about the interviews for the Head's position, Bob.'

'Ah yes, I suppose we need to put some flesh on the bones regarding the structure of the day. Now Ken Grayman, the Acting Deputy Head, will be the best person to help with the timetable of panel meetings and interviews; he's very good at that sort of thing. As I'll be one of the candidates, I shouldn't have anything to do with the arrangements, but you know me, Dorothy, I'm always here to lend a hand.'

Why is she looking at the floor? Why is she avoiding my gaze?

'Is everything okay Dorothy?'

'You've not been short-listed, Bob. The Board of Governors wanted me to thank you for the stalwart job you've done in holding the reins since Ted Shilling's tragic departure. They wanted me to pass on their gratitude for all that you've done and hope you will give your full support to the new Headteacher, whoever he or she may be.'

I'm lost for words. I cannot believe what I've just heard. I'm the acting Head forchristsake!

'Surely there's some mistake, Dorothy,' I start to say, more in hope than expectation. 'I thought I'd done enough to warrant at least a place amongst the candidates.'

Dorothy tries to smile and look sympathetic at the same time. She need not have bothered. The muscles controlling her smile are so obviously under-used and underdeveloped all she manages to do is imply she is about to break wind.

'We felt the school needed fresh blood and a new direction. Recent results have not improved in line with Government targets, as you well know.'

'I know what the statistics say,' I begin; an introduction to my best "it's not my fault" speech, 'but there's more to running a school like this than numbers on a database or ticks in a box. There's passion, drive and the desire to create the very best educational experience for every pupil here at Laburnum High. This is not just about having good challenging lessons, this is about understanding what makes a good citizen and how we, as professionals, can help to nurture this quality in all our pupils.'

'Our last OFSTED inspection said we were not challenging the pupils enough. They said our management was weak and our staff lacked direction,' she said, reading from a note pad. She was damn well reading from a note pad! 'They also said our provision for Citizenship was not good whilst our methods for tackling underachievement needed a complete overhaul.'

'We know there is a job to do,' I offer, feebly.

'The interviews will take place two weeks today. I assume I can count on you to make all the necessary arrangements and see that everyone is well taken care of? Here is the candidate list.' These are her final words as she drops a sheet of folded A4 paper on to my desk and leaves.

Linda enters with a tray of coffee.

'I'm sorry Mr Pike, but we only have Bourbons. All the Hobnobs went at the parents' evening last week.'

The PA leaves the tray on my desk and goes. I sit staring at the plate of long dismal brown biscuits; my least favourite of all time. I feel like one of those biscuits left at the bottom of the box, discarded, unwanted, stale and unpopular. I bring my fist crashing down on the plate and crush the Bourbons with one clean hit just as Ken Grayman, Acting Deputy Headteacher and full-time pillock, walks in.

'Hello Bob,' he says jauntily, a plastic garden gnome grin moulded on to his flabby face.

Apparently, he fancies himself as a bit of a sportsman but with his physique, size and looks he reminds me more of a Spacehopper than a hard-bodied athlete; either way, he's a trumped up little snot at the best of times.

'What is it Ken? I'm very busy right now.'

He ignores my feeble attempt to remain in a state of depressed solitude and takes up residence in the seat just vacated by the Judas of Governors.

'Oh, I just saw Dorothy Biggar leaving and was wondering if anything has been decided about the interviews for the Head's job?'

I look at him. His bouncy, jaunty demeanour is revolting. How he ever became a Deputy Head, even an acting one, is a complete mystery to me.

'She brought the candidate short-list in,' I reply.

'I expect you'll want me to organise the day?'

'No Ken, I'll organise it myself.'

'But surely you'll be on the short-list? How can you...? You are on the short-list, aren't you, Bob?'

The little shit knows. How the hell does he do that? He always seems to know about the Governors' decisions before I do. Maybe the rumours I've heard about him are true.

'No, I'm not on the short-list. I withdrew my application. I thought long and hard about it and finally decided the school needs new blood, a new direction, a different hand at the helm.'

'I thought it was your ambition to be the permanent Head here?'

The smug sod thinks he's being clever rubbing it in like this.

'Sometimes you need to place ambition to one side for the good of all those children out there. The school needs a new focus and I don't think I'm the man for the job in this case. Besides, the Governors have a strong field to select from and I'm sure they'll find the right candidate,' I say as I hold up the folded sheet of A4 paper.

'Is that the short-list?'

'Yes, she left it with me.'

'Do you mind if I take a look to see if I recognise any of the names?'

I give him the sheet. He opens it and almost immediately, I see the slight twitch of a smile flash across his podgy pockmarked features.

'Do you recognise any of the field?'

He shakes his head. Is he trying not to laugh?

'Not much of a field,' he finally says and then the smile develops in to a broad self-satisfied 'Cheshire Cat' grin.

I reach out and snatch the paper back from him. There is one name on the paper and one name only. It sits on the paper mocking me with every syllable, Ms Katherine Lowbridge.

I arrive home at just after six in the evening; it has not been a good day. Following the revelation of the short-list there was a fight in the English corridor, an irate neighbour complaining of broken windows and the arrest of a truanting pupil for shoplifting in a city department store. I've had my fill of dealing with parents, police, pupils and pissed-off teachers. All I want now is a comfortable chair and a bottle of red.

I park the BMW on the drive and go in the house. Valerie is nowhere to be seen and then I notice the backdoor is slightly open. My wife is in the garden. It is a lovely early spring evening and she will be tending her beloved roses. I go outside and stand on the patio to survey my castle's kingdom. It is a wonderfully organised and cultivated garden. Val is an excellent gardener and in her hands, things grow firm and healthy. As predicted, she is busy fussing over her darling roses. She is bending over with her back to me. She wears a light summer print dress of a softly flowing silky material that helps to emphasise the beautiful curve of her delightful buttocks; she is still one hell of a woman. She gently wiggles as she strategically snips at the stalks of a bush and this stirs a reaction below my equator.

The garden is a secluded place and we are not overlooked. I creep up behind her and stealthily begin to lift her dress. She is wearing a skimpy pair of pink lace panties, the only remaining barrier between me and several moments of sheer ecstasy.

8

'Bob, what do you think you're doing? And in broad daylight,' she exclaims as she stands and turns to face me, brandishing a savage looking pair of pruning shears, her delightful rear slipping out of my grasp and back beneath the sanctity of the flimsy dress; the moment is lost, the reaction subsides. 'You should do things like that in the bedroom, not out here in the garden.'

'They're not going to interview me for the Head's job. They said I wasn't up to the task of leading the school.'

Val drops the pruning shears, throws her arms around my neck and plants a big wet kiss on my cheek.

'Oh you poor, poor dear, why on earth did they do such a horrible thing?'

'They're only going to interview one person for the job. I think it's a stitch up.'

'Oh, don't be so silly! Things like that don't happen in education. I'm sure there's a perfectly good reason why they've only chosen one person.'

'Sometimes, Val, you're just so naive.'

At the end of the day in bed, I dream. I dream I am falling, falling past crumbling towers of marble, falling past shattered mountains. I fall and fall until I see Laburnum High School below me getting closer and closer. My rapid descent begins to slow and eventually I come to rest in a seat opposite the desk in my office. In my chair, the Head's chair, sits a dragon of fearsome countenance, casually signing cheques in the school bank account chequebook.

Upon noticing my presence, the foul and hideous creature roars at me belching mouthfuls of searing hot flames from its fetid maw. My clothes are instantly turned to cinders and I stagger back with the force of the blast, yet I miraculously survive for beneath my vaporised clothing I wear a brilliant shiny suit of the most exquisite armour. I draw my sword and take up my shield, emblazoned with the image of a white Laburnum tree, and advance upon my foe. The mighty dragon draws itself up to its full height and spreads its massive wings, in doing so the monster reveals her sex. We begin to circle each other looking for the first opportunity to strike.

'Come let me embrace you in my arms,' she hisses.

'Go to hell you spawn of the Devil,' I defiantly reply. 'I intend to smite you down and take back my crown.'

We charge at each other and our battle to the death commences.

CHAPTER 2

BROKEN BOILERS AND INVESTMENT OPPORTUNITIES

"And Babylon shall become heaps, a dwelling place for dragons, an astonishment, and a hissing, without an inhabitant."

Bible quote

For about the umpteenth time this year I'm told by my site manager that the school needs a new main boiler. Time was when a caretaker, the former name of all site managers, would simply fix the old one uncomplainingly and expect no reward for his labours except an acknowledgement of his undoubted prowess in dealing with all things technical. Nowadays they justify their position as an SM by sitting on their fat arses in little offices, spending vast amounts of school budget hiring contractors to change a light bulb or fix a blocked sink. The world has truly grown pampered and soft now this once steadfast and noble breed has evolved in to nothing more than a glorified paper pusher.

'I just want it recorded that our boiler will not last another winter,' says Tom Lavender, a huge great ox of an individual with an acute case of halitosis and lead-penetrating body odour.

'Duly noted, but may I say that you said exactly the same last year,' I remind him, 'and the year before that and the year before that. In fact, you've told us the same thing for the last seven years and our answer has always remained unchanged; we do not have the money to replace the boiler, Tom. You'll just have to see if you're capable of fixing it yourself.'

I can see from his eyes how my tactic successfully challenges the creature hidden inside him; the one not dependant upon and controlled by paperwork and bureaucracy. If this is what it takes to release the suppressed spirit of the caretaker, then so be it.

'Well I suppose I could have a look at it myself,' he says.

'And I'm sure you'll find a way to keep the old thing working through another winter, as only a man with your expertise could. In return you would have earned the admiration of yours truly as well as the thanks of the Governors, staff and pupils of the school.' Instantly I see I have won this minor skirmish. 'We are very lucky to have someone with your technical skills looking after us all.'

He leaves my office sporting a broad, self-satisfied smile. It's the last I'll hear of the boiler until next year when we will play out the scene once more; surely, one year he will not be so easy to convince, or perhaps the boiler will actually break down for good. That is not my concern; it will be the decision of the new Head by then. In other words, who gives a toss!

With this thought comes a tightening of my gut, a clenching of my fists and a vibration from my bowels. Am I really going to lose this office, this desk, the power? Am I really going to become subservient to Ms Katherine bloody Lowbridge?

A knock at my door snaps me from my melancholia.

'Toby Marriott wants to know if he can see you urgently,' says Linda Hewlett, as she peeps around the edge of the door.

I am about to say I do not have the time to spare, but she is adept at reading my body language and fires another salvo before I've had time to intercept the first.

'He says it's a matter of life and death and insists you really will need to speak to him.'

Teachers come in all shapes and sizes. Some are more efficient, some are more creative. Some fight for the cause of cynicism while others are champions of enthusiasm and commitment. I've known many teachers truly dedicated to the belief they can really make the difference to a young persons life, but I've also met a considerable amount that don't give a fig and regard each day as one closer to retirement and escape from the intolerable environment of the classroom. Very few teachers are what you would call unique, but Toby Marriott would certainly come close to earning that rare accolade.

I've known him since he joined the school as a newly qualified teacher six years ago and in that time he has been a magnet for trouble; a receptacle for all things incongruous in a teacher's character. The problem with Toby Marriott is simple; he cannot keep his pet "bed snake" in his trousers. He is renowned as a ladies man, a rake, a Don Juan, a gigolo, rampant sex junkie and, given the chance, a despoiler of all things virtuous. Up until now, if the rumours are to be believed, he has ruined the lives or marriages of several female members of staff. I expect his current predicament was ready waiting in the wings to make an unwelcome entrance.

'You've done what?' I exclaim, after I have given him adequate time to explain to me his "life and death" situation. It's as I expected, he's got involved with a pupil. 'You bloody fool. You stupid bloody fool!

It is easy to see why he has women falling at his feet. He is classically good looking with a shock of blonde hair. He is always tanned and fit and takes good care of his body, if you discount most Friday and Saturday nights. Physically, you would think he'd have been the perfect graduate of the Hitler Youth. As you get to know him and dig beneath the shallow crust of self-interest and egotism you realise he is far and away more despicable than that.

'She was begging me, Bob; she damn well near threw herself at me and, well, she is almost eighteen.'

I stare at him, amazed at his pure arrogance and at his readiness to blame the situation on the naive pupil.

'She's not sixteen until next month and, more importantly she is a student at this school and as such demands our care and protection. You, on the other hand, are a teacher, a professional, a respected member of society, a role model and should be a bloody responsible adult!'

'But Bob, she approached me in the pub and the way she was dressed… well, any full-bloodied man would've probably done the same thing.'

'Don't delude yourself with that misplaced logic, Toby. You are, and always have been, a time bomb waiting to go off and now you tell me this girl's parents have found out that you have been having intimate relations with their daughter. Well, it seems you've finally stuck "it" in the wrong place. The law is quite specific on these matters. You realise I will have no alternative but to suspend you while a police investigation is carried out and the Governors' informed? I'm not going to pull my punches; almost certainly, you will be dismissed, but that doesn't mean there won't be other charges to face. That depends on how far the parents want to take this. You've been placed in a position of care and you have abused the trust placed in you. You'll never teach again, if I have my way.'

He drops his head into his hands and starts to weep. I hate to see a grown man cry, but I suppose it is understandable in a situation like this and besides I could never label Toby Marriott with anything remotely resembling maturity.

'Oh God, Bob. I'm so sorry!

The tears flow freely, perhaps too freely. Whatever the case I am not moved by them; Toby Marriott is a little shit about to get his just desserts. Soon the parents will contact me, probably the police then...

'Bob, is there anything I can do? Can I make amends somehow?'

Something deep inside me, a voice not stirred by sympathy or pity, calls out and tells me to stay the executioner's hand. The voice suggests that covering up Mr Marriott's sins could be an investment in my own future. Who knows, there may come a time when I need to call in favours from those significantly in my debt?

15

Although the voice makes a strong case for my intervention, I need time to think this through I must be certain I will not place my own good name in jeopardy. I make my decision.

'I know this girl. She's been a trouble maker throughout her time at this school and now, because she's developed an insatiable crush on you, she wants to hurt you because you've spurned her advances.'

Toby, perhaps a little too easily, stops the weeping and raises his head from the cradle of his hands.

'It's common for young girls to become infatuated with the younger male members of staff. We understand this, but false accusations can have a damaging effect on a teacher's career.'

'Yes,' he nods frantically. 'Yes. I told her to leave me alone, but she kept stalking me so I came to you to ask for help.'

'For which you are to be commended, Toby. The parents will be told that I have been monitoring the situation for some time and that you have acted in a forthright and professional manner.'

I pick up the phone handset and dial Linda's number. She answers as speedily as usual.

'Ah Linda, would you contact the parents of Kirsty Twain in year 11, please? I need to speak to them urgently.'

I replace the receiver. Toby still looks incredibly nervous and he should do, he deserves to. What I am about to do is for my benefit not his. If the truth were told, he should have taken his punishment there and then.

The phone rings and Linda informs me she has Mr Twain on the line. I thank her and then the game begins.

'Mr Twain, I'm glad I've been able to catch you. I have something I need to discuss with you. It's about your daughter...

It takes me about ten minutes to save Toby's career; it will take him a much, much longer span of time to pay me back.

'Bob, that was masterful,' he gushes, thinking I'll be impressed by his recognition and admiration of my diplomatic skills.

'Cut the bootlicking, sycophantic, claptrap. I'm not interested in your adulation. I've saved your hide and you owe me. One day I may require the favour returned. You get my meaning?'

'Yes, yes of course I do, Bob.'

'Also, this is your last chance. If I have any other complaints or hear any more about your sordid little encounters, I'll publicly castrate you myself. Understood?'

'Yes, Bob,' he answers obediently.

I dismiss him and he retreats from my office, but before he closes the door, I call him back.

'If you must insist on poking your disgusting pox ridden member into something connected with this school, then may I suggest the Head of English. Rumour has it she's been waiting for you to approach her.'

'She's not exactly my type if you know what I mean, Bob. She's a fat, ugly cow and almost twice my age.'

'Agreed, but you'll do as you're told, Toby. Besides, she's a bloody good teacher and I'd like her to stay here for the foreseeable future. You can give her reason not to go looking for new jobs. Be nice to her. Once or twice will do, at least until we've passed the resignation deadline for this year; then you can ditch the bitch.'

'Okay, Bob.'

He mutters something inaudible as he closes the door. I'm driven to thinking Toby will be a useful asset in the weeks and months ahead. His skill in unlocking every woman's knicker safe is a weapon I may have a use for now and again.

I've had a satisfying day today. As I drive home, I reflect on dealing with the old boiler problem, tackling the issue of keeping one of my best teachers, placating angry parents and, best of all, gaining a trooper I will undoubtedly require in the war to come. With less than one week to go before the interview for the permanent headship, I am as content as I can be.

I steer my big BMW onto the drive and I am soon in the hallway of my home.

'Is that you darling?' calls Val. 'I'm upstairs in the bedroom.'

This simple phrase uttered from her sweet lips is enough to cause a stirring in my groin. Hastily I mount the stairs in the hope there will be another mounting in the bedroom. The door is open; I am not disappointed. Val is pacing up and down wearing a lacy bra and knickers set complete with matching suspender belt, stockings and black high-heeled shoes. Feeling all my dreams have been answered I hastily release my erection from the confines of my trousers and charge into the room.

'Hi darling.' says Val as I enter the room. 'You know Monica, don't you? She's just started selling this range of glamour lingerie and asked me if I'd like to try it...'

I stand in the bedroom facing my own scantily dressed wife and her seated friend, Monica Dalrymple, from two doors away. Both women's eyes are fixed firmly on my crotch. Monica titters, Valerie screams. I wish I were dead.

I am alone, in bed at the end of the day. Val has decided to sleep in the spare room. The fallout from the argument that ensued following my exposure and Monica's speedy departure promises to last for many a day. Valerie feels she has been humiliated to an unprecedented degree; she may have a point. She was eager to point out that Colin Dalrymple is my regular golfing partner, as well as the biggest gossip in the club.

This thought is still firmly locked in my mind as I lose consciousness and drift off into an uneasy sleep.

Once more, I face the hideous, fire-spewing reptile I have fought for many nights and yet this time the great she-creature is not seeking to reduce my bones to cinders or crush my body in her mighty limbs. No, this time the monster is laughing at me. Rolling around on the floor, clutching her belly and laughing so much that she is on the verge of expelling every last drop of urine from her great fetid bladder. The she-beast points at me and I find I am surrounded by the population of Laburnum High: the staff the pupils and the Governors. They all begin to laugh and then point at me. I look down and discover I am naked below the waist and have an erection.

'Need some help in using that thing?' says Toby Marriott as he emerges from the crowd wearing matching black bra, pants and suspenders. 'How d'you want me, Bob? You know I'll do anything for you.'

I wake up screaming.

CHAPTER 3

MEDIAEVAL TREBUCHETS AND THE PURCHASER OF SOULS

*"The man who fights too long against dragons
becomes a dragon himself"*
Friedrich Nietzsche

It is the Friday before the interview for the headship of the school and I am attending a presentation by year nine pupils in the design and technology department.

Once upon a time, artisans dominated this sector of the school, practising their trade by instructing the male youth of society in the finer arts of making coffee tables and woven raffia-topped stools or casting aluminium garden forks. Nowadays the once steadfast bastions of woodwork and metalwork have been replaced by an airy-fairy sham of a subject called D&T. Generally this is staffed by a collection of silly young females skilled in the art of cutting out and sticking down pictures from the latest Argos catalogue, and over-the-hill males who have failed to hold on to their mundane little jobs in industry.

I have been invited to listen to a group of pupils lay out their detailed plans for a new group project inspired by their teacher, Mr Forrest.

The presentation was slickly done and illustrated by a well-prepared slide show projected from computer onto an interactive white board. The children demonstrated their knowledge of structures, forces and, for some reason, mediaeval weapons before getting down to the nitty-gritty of the project.

'This is where you come in, Sir,' said Benjamin Grimmet, the group's spokesperson and a dead-ringer for a five-foot intellectual gerbil. 'We'd like you to provide the finance for our project which we intend to construct after school and during our lunch and break times.'

'I'm listening,' I say, trying to sound interested whilst inwardly giving my answer as a resounding 'piss off' even before I understand the complete nature of the request.

Young Benjamin clears his throat then looks over to his teacher, Mr Forrest, for morale support.

'We need four hundred pounds to buy materials to build a fully working mediaeval French trebuchet.'

At that point one of his young compatriots hits a computer key which brings up the next slide on the big white screen; a set of detailed plans for a 13th century siege weapon.

'It's a sort of giant slingshot that could throw things at and over castle walls. Sometimes they would use huge boulders to smash the castle's defences and sometimes they would throw rotting carcasses of cattle into the fortress in the hope of starting a plague.'

I have had some weird requests for helping spend the school budget, but this probably counts as among the most bizarre.

'Well, I've certainly been impressed with your presentation, but before I can release those sorts of funds I'll need some time to think it over. In the meantime perhaps you could answer me a simple question.'

'Certainly,' says the eager, chubby-faced Grimmet.

'Why?'

'Ah yes, Mr Pike I think I can answer that one.' Derek Forrest finally enters the discussion and about time considering this is his project with the pupils merely being the puppets in seeing another of his demented notions put into action. Over the years, his charges have built everything from a twenty-foot radio-controlled replica of the Tirpitz to a 1:35th scale diorama of the Siege at Mafeking, complete with sound effects and miniature explosions. His fascination with all things military have coloured his thinking to such an extent that his fanaticism and enthusiasm has seduced countless cohorts of unsuspecting youngsters. Like some martial Pied Piper, he organises his adolescent troops to help engineer some of the most crackpot schemes and pass them off as "educational."

'You see, no one has ever built a working replica of this design. True, there have been a number of English trebuchet's constructed and, to my knowledge, one Austrian but never a twelfth century French "la Grande Terreur,"a true Rolls Royce of mediaeval siege weaponry.'

'Now I understand; it's all very clear. Once again, thank you all. Mr Forrest, perhaps you'd like to come to my office later and I will give you my decision personally.' It is only behind closed doors that I can tell him what a total lunatic he is and that there is not a hope in hells chance of me releasing such funds for his ridiculous scheme.

'Thank you Mr Pike. Will two o'clock be okay?'

I tell him that's fine then head off through the corridors back to my office. As I am walking through the area of the maths department I see a pupil standing outside one of the classrooms, obviously sent there as a punishment by the teacher. I decide to challenge him; it's a mistake I don't make too often.

'And why are you outside this classroom, young man?'

The boy looks at me as if I am nothing more than a dog-turd he has discovered attached to the sole of his shoe. No answer is forthcoming.

'I asked you a question, young man.'

Now he turns away, ignoring my presence entirely. I move into his visual range again and this time I am more assertive.

'What's your name? I've never seen you before. Are you a new pupil?'

'What's it to you? Who do you think you are?' he finally answers, not even bothering to make eye contact.

'What's it to me? Who do I think I am?' I'm staggered. No one has ever spoken to me like this before. 'My name is Mr Pike and I'm the Headteacher of this school.'

'That's a stupid name. Are you a fish or something?'

I'm angry now. I stopped to challenge him and within seconds he's wound me up to boiling point without breaking into a sweat himself. He's new, he must be, otherwise I would have crossed swords with him before. I'm about to take my actions to the next level and start issuing threats of punishment for insolence when the door to the classroom swings open and out rushes Mr Duddy, Head of Mathematics.

'Mr Pike, thank heavens you're here. This young man only started at the school this morning and already he's disrupted my lesson so badly I've not been able to teach. I've only just managed to get the others under control. The boy is intolerable.'

Calvin Duddy has always been a highly-strung individual, apt to fly off the handle at the slightest misdemeanour, but in this case I can understand his level of upset.

'Your lesson is crap and you can't teach it. Maths is crap and this school is crap and the teachers are all wankers,' spouts the lad, thus lighting Mr Duddy's touch paper for a second time.

'You see what I mean, Mr Pike. This boy should not be here. This school would be much better without boys like him,' he counters, pointing an accusing finger at the lad.

The boy, however, is a master tactician and his timing perfect. He delivers the killer blow.

'Yeah, and this school would be a whole lot better if they sacked useless teachers like you who rely on textbooks and computer programmes to do the teaching for them. When you talk to the class most of them are falling asleep. You're so boring. Why don't you quit and give someone else a chance?'

At this point I see my colleague is about to blow the proverbial gasket. I decide to defuse the situation and remove the boy from the vicinity of the maths department. I calm the teacher with promises that the matter will be dealt with and ask him to return to his class.

Once Mr Duddy is out of the picture I return my focus to the boy. He is smirking a smirk that suggests he is thoroughly pleased with his work.

'What is your name?' I ask once more in the vain hope he may reveal it to me.

'Daniel Webster,' replies the boy, in a matter-of-fact way.

'Well Daniel, I think you'd better come down to my office.'

Surprisingly he agrees, but then why shouldn't he? He's totally defeated his adversary and now he has the adventure of entering the Head's office to do battle with the biggest fish in the pond.

As we make our way to my office I decide to try and get the edge on the conflict to come. I call Shirley Makepeace on my mobile. Shirley is one of the very few teachers in the school for which I have any real respect. She is Head of the Special Needs department and has an encyclopaedic knowledge of every child in the school with problems. Not only that, but she also has a handle on every new arrival at the school.

By the time, I arrive at my office Shirley is already there with a large file of papers under her arm.

'I see you've met young Daniel, Mr Pike. What's he been up to this time?'

I quickly usher her into my office and instruct Daniel to wait. Once inside I am able to talk freely.

'This time? Bloody hell, the kid only started here today and already he has almost given Cal Duddy apoplexy. What else has he done?'

'He upset Karen Toombs in art and so she's gone home sick with stress and threatening to bring in her union if the boy remains in school.'

'My God, its only ten forty-five, he's been in the school two hours.'

'Well not quite,' replies Shirley. 'He was forty minutes late starting.'

Things seem to go from bad to worse. I ask Shirley to give me a breakdown of his previous history. It's then I begin to understand the sort of person I'm going to be dealing with.

'Daniel has a very troubled background. Up until six months ago, he'd been living with his mother and sister; not unusual until you discover they are one and the same person. He was recently placed in care when social services discovered his mother come sister was working as a prostitute to help fund her drugs habit. She has been beaten badly on several occasions by her pimp, who is also her father and the father of Daniel. Fortunately, this bastard went down for five years last month, but not before Daniel managed to threaten to kill him when he comes out.'

'Bloody hell,' is all I can muster as an intellectual response to the sad, sorry tale.

'Since being taken into care Daniel had been permanently excluded from two schools, Laburnum is viewed very much as his last chance. It's been one thing after another with Daniel,' continues Shirley. 'He's been arrested twice for shoplifting, has been accused of violent behaviour on several occasions, including trying to attack the man he knows to be his dad, and was even placed on remand for trying to break in to the police station where they were holding his mother. So you can understand why he's like he is.'

'And so why have we got him now?'

'You know the score Bob. When there's nowhere else to go, send them to Laburnum. We are, literally, his last chance. However, Daniel is also very bright and given the chance he could easily develop into university material.'

Shirley completes her pen portrait and leaves my office. I sit on my own thinking about the unfortunate way life has seen fit to treat young Webster. This is by no means common practice for me. Most people believe those in the teaching profession are there because they have an affinity for children and a desire to see young people succeed. Let me state now, this is definitely not the case, as far as I am concerned. I hold no such romantic notions about 'making the difference' or 'providing the perfect role model'. The reality is I couldn't give a toss about their chances of future success and I wholeheartedly prescribe to the theory that schools are much better places to work in when the kids aren't there. In fact, I would go as far to say that if I have contact with a child over the course of a week, I have failed in upholding my own personal ethos.

That being said, the case of young Webster does create an ember of sympathy in the usually icy cold non-child-friendly recesses of my heart. I decide I need to talk to the boy and call him into my office.

He looks more nervous and less self-assured now that he is on my turf, but I make him feel at ease as I have no wish to punish him.

'Take a seat Daniel. I'd like to talk to you.'

'What if I don't want to talk to you?' he says as he sits on the chair opposite my desk. 'I don't like talking to teachers.'

'I don't want you to think of me as a teacher, Daniel.' I certainly do not consider myself to be one. 'I want to see if there's anything I can do to help you settle in to Laburnum School.'

'Yeah, you can get them to let me live with my mom again for a start and you could give me some money so I can give it to her so that she can stop selling herself to the pigs she has to go with.'

In that one sentence he said more than any 'pen portrait' and accurately summed up all his problems. I look at him. His hands are grubby and his clothes, although clean enough, are shabby. His shoes have certainly seen better days. Although he displays all the trappings of poverty, his eyes contain a fire and intelligence that sing out his intention not to be beaten by this savage life. In him I see a young man that will meet his challenges head-on and refuse to submit to the cruel hand Fate has dealt him. I greatly admire him for that quality alone.

I know that sometime later today Calvin Duddy will come hammering on my office door demanding to know when and where I have arranged for the public flogging of this lad. He will threaten me with union intervention and demand satisfaction, but then coming from his safe, protected, middle class background, what else should I expect? We cannot begin to imagine the adversities this young man has suffered or the hardships he has yet to endure.

'From what I've been told, your mother is better off where she is for the time being and I'm sure you'll be reunited with her when she is released.'

He sneers at my words. It's almost as if he's heard these words a thousand times before. I decide, however, that as he's not heard them from me before I'll continue.

'I'll even use what power I have to help make certain you see your mom again soon.'

Now I have his attention.

'I'll do what I can to help you, Daniel, but you need to give us a chance.'

'Well you can make certain I'm not taught by idiots like that maths bloke, for a start,' he says and I finally see a way forward.

'I can do more than that,' I promise. 'I can create a special timetable for you and get you extra support during your maths lessons. You won't need to go to Mr Duddy's classroom again. I can also offer you an open door to my office. If, at anytime, you feel angry or if you just need someone to talk to then you can come down here and speak to me.'

At this point the same little voice inside me that stopped me from crushing Toby Marriott's career once more speaks up and suggests yet another unethical response to a situation. For some reason I am, again, encouraged by my inner self to recruit an ally to assist in an, as yet, undeclared war. 'Buy his soul!' shouts the voice. 'Bind him to you! Make him yours to command!'

What I do next is not something suggested or recommended in any educational tome and is, to the best of my knowledge, not a well-practiced strategy for dealing with disaffected school children. That being said, my hand reaches in to my inside jacket pocket and grasps my wallet. I pluck three crisp, fresh, twenty pound notes and hold them out to the lad without explanation.

He's not suspicious of my motives or too proud. He takes the money from me.

'Use it how you will, but be certain to get yourself some new shoes. Most importantly, make certain this remains our secret. If you can do this, I promise to do everything in my power to help you and your mom. If you need any more, just let me know; is that understood?'

'You won't get anymore trouble from me Mr Pike,' he says, 'and I'll even apologise to the art teacher and Mr Crappy.'

He knows how to play the game all too well. I think I'm much better off with him on my side.

'You mean Mr Duddy.'

'Whatever.'

It's exactly two o'clock when Derek Forrest knocks at my office door; there are few people I like to see less. He's a man in his early fifties who obviously imagines he still retains the boyish charm and good looks of some thirty years previous. He likes to think he is still a cheeky, adorable chap with a smooth tongue and a quip for all seasons. In reality, he has all the charm and charisma of a second-hand car dealer's crooked accountant's bent bookie.

The newly acquired tribal tattoo and gold earring do nothing but enhance his inherent seediness.

'Hello boss,' he says as he enters my room. 'I've come to get your answer about the money for the construction project. I know it might sound slightly barmy, but the kids are really up for it and I think it would get the school some good publicity. I can see it from your point of view; it must sound as if I've gone totally mad and well, if the school can't afford four hundred pounds then I completely understand, in fact I can shelve the project and...'

'When would you start building the thing?' I ask, interrupting his irritating prattle.

'Er, about September or October, at the start of the new school year, but I can...'

'You can have six hundred,'

'I can have six hundred?'

Thankfully, he shuts up.

'You can have the money as well as a little extra. Just make certain you see the thing through. Also, I want you to encourage Daniel Webster in 9L to join the project group, is that clear?' As I say this I move to the door and open it.

'Yes, certainly Bob,' he says, 'anything you say,' and, understanding the audience is over, he leaves the office.

'I'll inform the finance office to make the funds available to you.'

I close the door, the job is done. Another piece of the jigsaw is shaped in my mind. I could easily have squashed the ludicrous scheme, but why should I? Any problems resulting in the use of such a contraption will be 'Hers' to deal with and not mine.

I arrive home earlier on Friday than I do during the rest of the week. Valerie is sitting on the sofa in the lounge wearing a face pack and reading this month's edition of Garden and Home. She's still not speaking to me following my rude interruption of her lingerie party the other day.

I say hello, for which I obtain the expected zero response. I make my way into the kitchen to be confronted by an array of yellow sticky 'post it' notes, placed strategically around the room.

I pluck the nearest one from the hood of the cooker. Pasta bake for dinner - in the oven - heat up when needed, it says. By reading the rest of the informative yet annoying little messages, I learn that Val is going to spend the weekend with her mother in Grantham and that I'm expected to fend for myself while she is away. The last note I see is stuck to the pin board. It reads:

You'll have the house to yourself for the weekend, so you can walk around with your 'thing' hanging out all the time, if you wish. Just make certain you put it away for when I get back, just in case I have my mother with me.

Valerie.

CHAPTER 4

THE GOLF BALL OF FATE AND THE SHOULDER PADS OF POWER

"Those who seek absolute power, even though they seek it to do what they regard as good, are simply demanding the right to enforce their own version of heaven on earth. And let me remind you, they are the very ones who always create the most hellish tyrannies. Absolute power does corrupt, and those who seek it must be suspect and must be opposed."
Barry Goldwater

It's Sunday and I'm on the golf course with my playing partner, Colin Dalrymple. To give him his due, he has waited until the eleventh hole before he mentions the embarrassing situation witnessed by his wife the week before.

'I haven't seen you for a few weeks,' he says, as he tees off.

I place my ball on my tee and select a club, a three wood.

'I've been busy with various things.'

'So where do you hang out these days?' Even before he's finished his contrived line, he bursts out laughing. 'From what Monica told me, it's mainly in front of house guests.'

Now he erupts into fits of uncontrollable laughter, which causes me to totally fluff my shot.

'Oh bloody hell, Colin, now look what you've made me go and do. I'm in the sodding bunker.'

He gains control of himself, but only long enough to throw in another well aimed and practised jibe.

'Sorry, old man, I thought that you were only in the dog house with Valerie.'

'Very funny and now you've had your little laugh can we get on with the round?'

'Sure Bob, sure,' he says as we begin walking down the fairway towards our respective second shots. My ball is well and truly embedded in the sand under the lip of the biggest bunker on the course while his, with a perfect lie, is smack bang in the middle of the fairway.

'Do you want to forfeit some shots and drop your ball out of that sod?' he says, referring to my near impossible position in the sand trap.

'Bugger off. I'm not forfeiting anything. My trusty sand-wedge will do the trick.'

With that I take the club from my trolley and stride purposefully to where my ball is lying. I assess possible means of escape by estimating the angles and the direction I need to hit the ball. My best chance seems to be to aim for the semi-rough just to the left of the bunker. From there I will be able to see the green and have a decent chance of getting a par four for the hole. The only problem I can see with the shot is the large oak tree close by. If I hit the ball too hard I could be in an even worse position for my third shot as the ball could fall behind the great mass of trunk or get marooned in one of the deep pits and channels made by the massive root network close to the surface. However, having weighed up all the alternatives, this appears to be the only viable option.

Carefully and with all the poise and expertise of a real pro, I set my stance and go through several practise swings before preparing myself for the actual shot. I can feel in my water that everything is right; this will be a perfect shot. I raise the club to the top of its arc and I'm just about to allow my body to go through with the swing when Colin trumps up once more.

'Monica said your cock isn't very impressive.'

It's too late to pull out of the swing and I hit the ball far too hard. Like the space shuttle leaving Cape Canaveral, the ball zooms straight out of the bunker amidst a spray of flying sand. It travels at an incredible velocity and straight as the proverbial poker. Both of us watch in awe as, having bounced hard against one of the thick outstretched branches of the great oak, the ball ricochets back towards us.

Colin still has a beaming, broad grin etched across his features showing every one of his gleaming white front teeth. It's almost as if the golf ball is caught by some mystical magnetic attraction to the sparkling opalescence of his incisors as it terminates its rebound trajectory by colliding full on with his immaculate white smile.

Later, the specialist who examined Colin's devastated mouth tells me he is lucky to loose only eight front teeth, and that talking will be almost impossible for at least a week or two until the bruising, swelling and lacerations have healed. Colin will need to go through a painful and very expensive programme of reconstructive dental work.

By the time Monica arrives at the hospital Colin is away with the fairies in a morphine-induced sleep. I have to relate all the facts and in doing so I am pleased to spare none of the gory bloody details.

I leave the hospital a very happy man. It seems to me as though Fate has conspired to punish those that seek to profit at my expense. With that comforting thought I realise I am no longer daunted by the prospect of the interview the following day and my first meeting with the Lowbridge woman.

It's Sunday night and again I lie in bed alone. Valerie has decided not to return from Grantham until tomorrow. I miss her deeply and wish dearly that she were lying close to me now. My hope is that her mood towards me will have changed on her return and that once again we can share the intimacy of the bedchamber.

Our lovemaking had once been passionate and joyful, but in recent years her appetite for nocturnal gymnastics seems to have waned so much that all I can expect is an occasional Friday night frolic following her monthly yoga class and an overindulgence of red wine.

I drift off into a deep sleep and in the dream that follows I find myself once more confronted by the dragon. This time the creature is much bigger and towers miles up into the sky above the buildings of Laburnum School. It looks so powerful, so confident. The dragon sees me standing at its feet and guffaws a deep booming noise that seems like thunder to me. I am not scared and I do not attempt to run, for I have with me a weapon with which to conquer this creature.

I reach into my pocket and pull out the hard shiny white sphere and hold it high.

'In my hand I grasp the sacred golf ball of fate and with it I shall smite you from the face of the Earth you disgusting hell-beast!'

'I am too powerful for any man to defeat,' spits the great scaly dragon-bitch. 'How do you hope to conquer me with such a tiny object?'

With that the beast lowers its hideous head towards me, its wide mocking grin revealing rows and rows of huge razor sharp teeth. I see my opportunity and bring back my arm and throw the golf ball with all my might. The magical weapon flies from my fingers and rockets towards the creature's beaming smile.

With an explosion that sounds like a hundred great crystal chandeliers falling in unison and smashing on a marble floor, the golf ball ricochets around every inch of the dragon's cavernous great orifice, destroying every last tooth.

'Laburnum School is mine and you shall not take it from me!' I shout triumphantly.

It's Monday morning; the fateful day has finally arrived. The Governors assembled early at the school, all filled with a sense of their own importance. They are gathered together to appoint the new Headteacher and today they will decide the fate of Laburnum School.

I am not involved in the formal interview procedure, although I am booked to meet with the successful candidate for thirty minutes following the announcement that an appointment has been made. It's obvious the Governors do not want me to speak to Ms Lowbridge before she accepts the post.

Brooding, I spend the morning in my office awaiting news that the pillar of smoke has been spotted. At eleven-thirty there is a knock on my door and Dorothy Biggar, Chair of Governors, scuttles in. She looks highly pleased with herself: like a smug northern feline, that has just won a lifetime supply of condensed milk.

'Bob, I just wanted to tell you that the Governors have come to a decision and offered the post of Headteacher to Kath Lowbridge,' she spouts. 'And I'm pleased to inform you that she has accepted.'

'Oh, there's a surprise,' is all I can muster as an enthusiastic reply.

'So now we hope you can spend some time with Kath and answer any questions she may have about the school.'

Without even bothering to wait for any response the little woman spins around, opens my office door and calls to Ms Lowbridge who is just outside; that's when I see her for the first time.

She is immense, easily as tall as I am, but wide at the shoulder like an American football star. As she walks into my office, she seems to fill the doorframe. She pays me no heed as she struts to the centre of the office, but I can see she is scrutinising every detail of the room, every shelf, every book, every picture on the wall. Dorothy, who behaves like a small flying insect buzzing around the nose of some huge disinterested bison, introduces her to me as the newly appointed Head of Laburnum School, then flutters off out of the office. I am left standing facing my nemesis.

Her size has, I now see, been augmented by the clothes she wears. Her height is pushed near to six feet, close to that of my own, by wearing four- inch heeled boots. The shoulders of the dark business suit she has on are padded to such an extent that she looks huge and hunched. Her short-cropped hair stands, brush-like, on the top of her head reminding me instantly of a sadistic American Marine Drill Sergeant or an enthusiastic SS Officer. This woman has taken power dressing to the highest level as every aspect of her appearance has been contrived to convey dominance.

'Hi, my name is Bob Pike, I'm the Acting Head,' I say, deciding to break the icy waste that stands between us. 'I'm very pleased to meet you and if...'

'I know who you are,' she interrupts, 'so spare me the false bonhomie. You resent me being here and you probably hate my guts already, but that's understandable considering the Governors did not think you suitable for the job. You see, I've been appointed to sort out the mess your predecessor has made of this school; a mess which, has been successfully perpetuated by you, to great effect I would add.'

She looks around the office again.

'I'm going to give you a list of things to accomplish before I take up the reins in September; I'll drop in now and again before then to check on your progress. You can start by clearing all this crap out of here,' she says, indicating the paintings and mementos that adorn my office, 'and get it redecorated. I'll send you a colour chart with my preferred choice.'

Her gaze fixes on my desk.

'You can get that pile of junk put in the skip too. I want a glass-topped desk with a new computer and a Harvey Nicholls, black leather Captain's chair. You can order it over the internet.'

She gives me no time to respond.

'From now on you are my Deputy and nothing more. You can stop play-acting and calling yourself "Acting Head". That ends now. You will not allocate any more of the school budget; from this moment any decision will be first approved by me. You can contact me by mobile phone or internet. Now, is everything clear to you?'

'Er, yes, I think so.'

'It had better be because I'll hold you responsible for anything untoward that happens here before I arrive.'

Casually she picks up my desk diary and starts to flip through it.

'When I arrive in September I intend to make some desperately needed cutbacks. Any weak staff, any non-essential personnel and any member of school management not pulling their weight will go.'

Almost on cue the door opens and Dorothy Biggar flutters back in.

'Have you two got to know each other? Are you both clear about things?'

'Yes,' I answer flatly

'Absolutely,' replies the she-beast.

As I drive home I reflect on the day and my first meeting with the man-hating, man-eating, Lowbridge creature. She is, indeed, a formidable adversary; perhaps even too great for me to handle. My earlier confidence has been shattered. I lament on my pathetic subservient performance in response to her dominating whirlwind of an introduction. Put simply, she treated me as if I were totally incompetent and has stripped me of any power I might have had. The warning was loud and clear; she will be gunning for me from September. Why did I let myself be spoken to in that way?

As I steer my big BMW onto the drive I promise to never let such a thing happen again. It is a promise I should have considered after I parked the car, for due to my lack of concentration I fail to see Val's new little green Mini sitting quietly halfway up the drive. I hit the thing full on and the BMW shudders to an abrupt, crunching stop.

Both cars are badly damaged, the Mini especially so. The little green car is Val's pride and joy. I stand still, staring at the wreckage, as she comes running out of the house. She takes one look at the state of her vehicle then turns and delivers a savage stinging slap across my left cheek.

'You bastard!' she screams. 'You bloody, bloody bastard!'

CHAPTER 5

THE BULLFIGHTERS ASSISTANT
AND BARBECUED RUMP

"...perhaps all the dragons of our lives are princesses who
are only waiting to see us once beautiful and brave.
Perhaps everything terrible is in its deepest being
something helpless that wants help from us."
Rainer Maria Rilke

The last few weeks before the summer holiday were pure
purgatory. Life with Val completely deteriorated.
Following the collision with her Mini, she moved out of
the bedroom on a permanent basis, taking all her clothes
out of the wardrobes and removing every item of hers
from drawers and dressing table tops; a feat which took
the best part of four days, plus a special consultancy
document and a risk assessment provided by Pickfords.
She even refused to come on holiday to our villa in
southern Spain, preferring to go to north Devon with her
mother.

At school, things fared no more positively. My life had
been made a constant misery by the incessant badgering of

"that woman" and the ridiculous tasks she insisted on setting me. It was easy to figure out her tactics; she was trying to wear me down, push me close to the edge so when the time came for the final nudge, there will be little left to do. What she doesn't realise is that I am fully aware of these tactics, having used them to my own advantage on several occasions. To her chagrin, I did every one of her stupid little tasks on time and efficiently. She tried to pressurise me and she failed; she severely miscalculated my character and my fortitude.

Most people assume I am an affable, easygoing bloke, with no real ambition or desire for power. They are, of course, wrong on every count. I adore power. I have many ambitions, all connected to my status as a school leader. More than ever, it is my desire to be the substantive Headteacher of Laburnum High and I aim to make certain I fulfil that desire.

I intend to put the weeks here in Spain to good use. It is here I will develop my strategy for dealing with that brush-topped Amazonian. It is here I will plan her downfall as I have plenty of time to develop the perfect strategy. I'll also need to take some time out, enjoy myself and make the most of the vacation.

I'm living here alone and the only time I see anyone is when I have friends around for a drink or decide to put on a barbeque. Fortunately, I've been coming here for years and have built up quite a circle of friends; when I'm feeling in a party mood I can easily pack them in. The only trouble is Val is usually the organiser of such events; her natural gift as a hostess is invaluable at such times. However, I am not going to allow myself to sit here fretting about such a thing; that's why I have arranged a barbeque party for this afternoon and invited a whole bunch of friends and neighbours.

In the kitchen, I set about chopping, washing and peeling the ingredients for the salad with, hopefully, the same precision and expertise as my absent wife. As I go about this chore my mind flicks to the last meeting I had with 'Her Majesty Lowbridge' before the school broke up for the summer…

'I'd like to meet with you a few times during the holiday. What are your plans?' she asked, with more than a little *whatever plans you have you'll need to change to suit me* in her voice.

'I go away for four weeks. I always go away for four weeks. We have a villa in the south of Spain. I've been going for the past eight years.'

She shook her head from side to side, as if she disbelieved each and every word entering her ears.

'Listen Mr Pike, you are a senior leader of this school and as such I expect you to be available whenever required to discuss school business. I take one week off in the summer and for the rest of the time I will be here in school preparing for the new educational year. How can you hope to have things organised by sunning yourself in Spain for four weeks?'

'When we come back from Spain we take my Mother-in-Law to Torquay for five days,' I added. 'It's almost a tradition; we've been doing it for the last ten years.'

'What?' came her instant, shocked response. 'You're unavailable for five out of the six weeks?'

'I'm afraid so, in fact I usually only pop in on the Friday before term starts, just so I can meet with the team and prepare for the new year.'

'How ridiculous!' she erupted. 'That will need to change. If I were you, I'd see what you can do about changing your travel dates.'

Of course, I refused and what followed was a heated debate about the responsibilities of a school leader. She threw at me facts about the amount of time needed to finalise structures for the first week back in school, while I struck back with the need to recharge my batteries and take quality time away from the workplace in order to be at my most able for the forthcoming year ahead.

When it ended, there was no clear winner. She thought she was right, whilst I knew I was. She abused her authority and threatened to take the matter further when we returned. I held on to the moral high ground and warned her about challenging me on such an issue.

A sharp pain brings me back to the present. I look down at the chopping board and realise that I have cut my finger badly.

All the guests have arrived and are tucking in to the ample supply of food and booze I have provided. Eamon and Grace Wagstaff, my nearest British neighbours are here, as are Roger and Penny Beaumont from the village close by. Paco and Silvia, a Spanish couple with an immaculate command of English, have come along with Hetty and Barbara Jakelin, two sisters who own and run a small café in the village. Paco is their supplier of fresh vegetables. The last to arrive were Geoff and Candice Huff who have brought a friend of theirs along.

When Candice introduced me to Juanita Cortez I was immediately smitten. This petite, golden skinned, black-haired Andalucian beauty instantly seduced me with her impish smile and caressed me with her intoxicating perfume; from the first second of our meeting I wanted her.

Fortunately and, I thought, miraculously, Juanita has been all too eager to spend time in my company. I'm sitting on a sun-lounger at the side of the pool as Juanita walks seductively towards me carrying two ice-cold beers fresh from the fridge.

'May I join you?' she asks as she takes up residence next to me.

She is so wonderfully gorgeous. Her close proximity and her aroma send hormones racing through my body. I want to reach out and hold her, pull her to me and make desperate, passionate love to her. That would be fine with me, but I'm not certain my guests would appreciate the two of us going "at it" ten to the dozen while they are tucking in to their chicken wings and pork sausages.

'Tell me about you,' I say, trying to sound calm while inwardly bursting with desire.

'I am visiting my friends, Geoff and Candice,' she says, in a heavily accented English. 'I meet them when they live in Seville.'

'And what do you do for a living?'

She doesn't understand my question so I try again.

'What work do you do?'

'Oh, trabajo, si, I understand now,' she says, and radiates her wonderful smile at me. 'I am an ayudante de torero, in English you would say a bullfighter's assistant. I work and travel all over the country with the famous El Elegido.

'El Elegido?'

'Si. El Elegido, the Chosen One.'

'Oh, that's a good ... er ... modest name.'

Her sensuous lips caress the tip of the beer bottle as she begins to sip the cool golden liquid. Even this simple innocent action triggers explosive chemical reactions in my body and I feel a movement in my swim-shorts.

'What do you do for work?'

Her question snaps me from the erotic thoughts that were beginning to flood through my mind. What work do I do? Hell's bells, she's just told me she travels all over Spain working with a sporting superstar. I can't possibly just say I'm a Headteacher. Where's the mystery and romance in that? No one here knows what I do for a living; over here no-one seems to care. Geoff and Candice, Juanita's close friends, definitely have no idea. I'm on safe ground; I can be who I like.

'I work in the movie business.'

'In the movies? That is so exciting!' she exclaims and I feel her body shift ever so slightly closer to mine so that our bare thighs touch.

'What do you do in the movies? Are you an actor?'

Now I realise the hole that I have started to dig for myself could well become so big I may never get out. If I tell her I'm an actor the next thing she'll be asking what films I've been in, then the names of the characters' and then whether they are available on DVD. I'm a total idiot, but there's no stopping now.

'I'm a stuntman.'

'A stuntman? Oh, you mean all those fights and car crashes? Muy bien, hombre! That is fantastico; I have never met a stuntman before.'

She seems more than impressed and I feel her thigh press harder against mine. I can't believe this is happening to me. I decide to try and change the subject now, while I'm ahead of the game with my stuntman story.

'It seems that we both do exciting work. Tell me, what's it like working for El Elegido; the Chosen One.

'He likes to think he is the greatest living bullfighter and a real hero of all the women in Spain.' She breaks her sentence to take another seductive sip of beer. 'Actually he's a real wanker.'

I burst out laughing at hearing her use such a word. She looks puzzled.

'Is that not right? Is it not wanker?'

'No, no, it's right. It's just that I didn't imagine anyone as sweet as you could use such words,' I reply quickly so as not to offend her.

'Maybe I am not so sweet, I think.'

'What do you mean by that?'

'Later,' she answers as she slides a soft cool hand down the inside of my thigh and blows a delectable little kiss at me. 'Later caballero,' she says again before standing up and skipping off to talk to Geoff and Candice over at the far side of the pool.

Am I dreaming? Have I just been transported to a world of fantasy, or has this sexy little Spanish vixen just made a pass at me? What does she mean by later? I decide to ease back on my consumption of alcohol just in case 'later' means what I hope it means.

It's been a long afternoon of chat, food and wine, but now my guests are beginning to say their farewells and make their way back to their respective haciendas. Geoff and Candice are the last to say goodbye, and for one horrible moment I imagine Juanita is going with them.

'We'll see you around old buddy,' says Geoff. 'It's been a great afternoon. Good to see the gang again.'

'Yes, you must come over to ours next time. It's a shame about Val, but perhaps next year?'

'Yes, I'm sure.'

She's standing with them as I desperately try to think of some way of keeping her with me. She came with them and so she'll go back with them.

I need not have worried; she obviously has everything in hand.

'I am staying to help Robert clear up the mess,' she says. 'He will drive me back later. Is this not true Robert?'

'What? Yes, si, yes, help me, of course, yes!'

Geoff looks at Candice who flashes a knowing smirk at her husband. Juanita is already off collecting plates and glasses.

'Okay, well that's settled then,' says Geoff. 'Just remember not to drop her back too late; she needs her bed time, old man.'

With this last cryptic statement he winks at me then he and Candice walk over to their big 4x4 and within seconds they are thundering up the dirt track away from my villa. I turn around to see the delicious Juanita standing, hands on hips, looking at me.

'It is hot,' she says, 'and it is time we had a swim.'

She bends down to grab the hem of her flimsy dress and slowly begins to raise it, pulling it over her head; she's totally naked beneath.

'Come here, Robert,' she commands.

Obediently I walk towards her, unable to take my eyes from her.

'You must take off these clothes,' she says and starts to pull my tee shirt up. I take over and quickly remove it, but as I haul it over my head I feel my swim shorts yanked down. For one brief moment the English prude within me wants to protest, but the Latin lover I yearn to be gains ascendancy and gives me better council.

I feel her hands caressing and massaging my manhood. I could explode then and there, but Juanita is too skilled and she understands how far to go, taking me to the brink then easing back.

'I think you need to cool down, hombre,' she whispers in a seductively husky voice before she releases her grip and jumps into the pool. She screams playfully as her delightfully petite golden body strikes the cool water.

'Now you jump in, Robert!'

I hesitate for one moment then launch myself in to the pool. I dive under and as I swim beneath the surface I see her naked form suspended in the clear water, her perfect breasts bobbing up and down rhythmically to the ebb and flow of the water. I swim up to her, but she wants to be playful and she dives beneath me; she's incredibly fast and agile in the water. As she passes beneath me I feel her soft hand stroke my genitals. The feeling makes me gasp for breath and I break through the surface coughing and spluttering.

I wipe the water from my eyes and look down to Juanita, still under the water and close to me. I see her head, her long black hair spread out. She strokes my thighs and then her mouth makes contact and again I feel as if I will burst. Seconds later she breaks the surface, a big smile on her face.

'Do you like the games I play in the pool?' she asks.

'Yes, oh yes I do.'

'Then we play more.'

She dives beneath the surface again and I dive under after her but she is too quick and she swims away towards the end of the pool. When she surfaces again she treads water, tempting me to catch her. I encircle my arms around her, but she slithers free and is off again. As the game continues I am driven to a point of near frenzy. As if sensing this she climbs out of the pool and stands on the edge and beckons me to join her. I need no second asking and hastily I climb out of the pool.

'I think you want to play another game now, eh Robert?' she says teasingly, pointing at my groin.

I want her now and I move towards her. I expect her to run but this time she waits and allows me hold her. We kiss passionately and my eager hands begin to explore her body.

Eventually she pulls away, even though I refuse to let go my grip.

'We need to go in the shade, Robert,' she says, 'the sun is very hot.'

She's right; the sun will bake us dry if we stand here much longer. Without asking permission I scoop her up in my arms and she gives a whoop of delight. I carry my beautiful prize to the shade of the canopy and as I put her down she reaches up and kisses me again, with even more passion than before, then she turns and bends over the large table we keep under the sun shade.

'Now my big bull, I am yours; take me!'

I need no further invite. I am ready waiting and eager to enter her. Looking down at her perfect body should be all I need to occupy my mind, but for some perverse reason my mind flicks and I see Lowbridge in the same bowed position. The gargantuan proportions of "her" have replaced Juanita's petite form.

Instead of the firm golden-skinned buttocks, I see a wobbly grey backside, two massive blotchy cheeks separated by a huge great hairy crevice.

'C'mon man, do your duty; I haven't got all day,' she commands. 'This is your next task. Let's see if you can do this one properly.'

The horrific image in my head deflates my sex instantly. Immediately my mind is infiltrated by worries of inadequacy and I am soon babbling apology after apology, but Juanita shows no sign of disappointment, once more takes charge, and rescues me from the effect of my fearsome fantasy.

'Oh, my big bull is not ready,' she pouts. 'Let me talk to him.'

She bends down and her mouth begins to work its magic. In no time, I have forgotten all images of Ms L and I am once more able and very willing to perform.

Juanita gyrates her hips expertly and I hold on to them while I move back and forth. I can feel the heat of the still hot barbecue warming my buttocks.

'Faster, faster, rapido!' she screams as our movements become more frantic. 'Hey! Mi gran toro, el amor conmigo, me quieres duro.'

She orders me to push harder and as I reach my own point of rapture I feel her body begin to spasm. Her perfect breasts sway to our rhythm; I close my eyes and allow my body to release its passion.

She is screaming and I am cursing as we push our bodies hard together. I feel myself release and flow inside her. I open my eyes, my ardor spent.

Val is standing staring at us, a suitcase in one hand and her flight bag over her shoulder; the look in her eyes is one of hatred, shock, horror and revulsion all combined. Behind her I can see a taxi, wending its way from the villa up the dirt track.

'You bastard!' she screams. 'You bloody, bloody evil cheating bastard!'

Juanita needs no further instruction to make her exit and she runs off; probably to get her clothes and head up the dirt track in the same direction as the taxi.

Val drops her case and flight bag and makes a b-line for me, her hand raised to strike. I know what's coming and this time I step back to evade the blow. Unfortunately, I've forgotten the close proximity of the barbecue. It's only when my buttocks come to rest on the scalding hot steel grill that I realise a slap to the face would have been eminently preferable as a punishment.

Later, the surgeon who tends to my wounds tells me the burns will take a number of weeks to heal properly and during that time sitting down will be very painful.

Val was kind enough to see that I was being cared for before she said she was leaving me and would be catching the next flight home.

Three days later Geoff and Candice come to visit me at the villa. Candice looks fairly sympathetic while Geoff finds it hard to contain his amusement.

'My God, how on earth did you manage to sit on the bloody barbeque?' he asks, but his voice betrays the fact that he knows the whole story.

'Geoff, don't be such an arse,' says Candice. 'Juanita told us all about it. We blame ourselves for bringing her. She's the same everywhere we go; the woman's absolutely man-mad.'

I didn't see Juanita again during the holiday. I would have liked to, but my injuries prevented me from socialising with anyone for the rest of my stay in Spain.

At the end of the vacation I sit, in a considerable amount of discomfort, on the aeroplane heading back home to England and reflect on the events of the last few weeks.

'Would you like anything to eat or drink?' says the young flight attendant, snapping me from my reverie.

'What do you have?' I ask.

'We have a very good barbequed pork and salad baguette.'

'No thanks.'

CHAPTER 6

TOO MANY HEADS SPOIL THE MISSION STATEMENT

"I suppose leadership at one time meant muscles; but today it means getting along with people."
Mahatma Gandhi

'Mr Pike, will you please sit down,' she commands me for the third time.

For the third time I explain yet again.

'I told you, I can't sit down because I had a slight accident on holiday and to do so would be very painful, so if you have no objections I'll stand.'

'Oh, but I do have objections,' she counters. 'This is a leadership meeting and I expect everyone to sit down and since you refuse to explain what injuries you suffered I have no alternative but to insist; now please get a chair and put up with the pain for the short time the meeting will last.'

She will not back down and she will not be happy until she's seen me in agony perched on a chair.

Tentatively I sit down and join the other school leaders gathered around the table. The leadership team is made up of six people including Lowbridge and myself. The others are Ken Grayman, once the Acting Deputy Head, now demoted to the strangely titled role of Assistant Headteacher; the same level of responsibility as Shirley Makepeace and Bill Anthony. The final member of the leadership team is Glenys Cooper, a Trainee Headteacher, but in actual fact more of an assistant Assistant Headteacher.

I have never quite been able to understand why there is this desire in education to change the names of jobs on such a frequent basis. The current crop of titles must be massively confusing to an outsider.

Until a few years ago it was simple, there was the Headteacher, the Deputy Headteacher and then a couple of senior teachers. These were the people entrusted with running the school. Everything was fine and people knew who was who. That was until some monumental idiot of a bureaucrat, decided that although you should still have the Headteacher and Deputy, you also required Assistant Headteachers, an Associate Headteacher, an Executive Headteacher, a Trainee Headteacher and a Trainee Assistant Deputy Headteacher. Even I would find it difficult to draw a hierarchy diagram explaining the relationships between this team. If I find it confusing, imagine the problems faced by the poor parent ringing the school to talk to the Headteacher...

'Hello, can I speak to the Headteacher please?'

'Yes certainly,' the helpful receptionist would reply; but only if you had stayed the course and listened to the plethora of digitalised recorded claptrap waiting for the unsuspecting member of the public when they contact a school. 'And which Headteacher would that be, the Assistant, the Deputy, the Executive, the Associate, the Trainee, the Substantive, the Acting or the totally bewildered?'

Why on earth change a system that was perfectly acceptable?

The stinging pain in my buttocks makes it difficult for me to focus on what Lowbridge is prattling about. When I do manage to get comfortable enough to listen I realise the pain may have been preferable.

'First of all I want to lay out my vision for Laburnum School. It is a clear message that will be understood by the pupils, parents, governors and staff of the school. In other words, all of our stakeholders. It is a short and succinct statement.'

She pauses for effect and Ken, Bill and Glenys nod their approval, as is their way. They still have career moves to make and want to ingratiate themselves early. Only Shirley, to her credit, retains an air of "heard it all before, yawn, yawn!"

She goes on.

'The common thread of effective leadership is the ability to motivate and inspire others, to commit to a common purpose and then to create the conditions that will enable them to succeed in achieving their goals. To do this I will ensure that leadership and management in all areas of the school will be supportive, developmental, and progressive and seek to encourage innovation. I will ensure that teachers are motivated to improve their own teaching skills, given opportunities to enhance their careers and encouraged to develop their abilities as training providers.'

And on…

'There will be a clear focus on learning and teaching. Practice will be reviewed on a regular basis. Middle leaders will be trained as learning and teaching coaches thus enabling high quality return in the sharing of good practice. Assessment will be regular and relevant and inform the setting of realistic and challenging targets. Students will be encouraged to develop as independent learners and must be encouraged and able to self-evaluate their progress.'

And on...

'Students will be given the opportunity to develop their collective voice and help develop practice within the school. As an ambassador and the senior professional I will work closely with the Governors to provide clear vision, leadership, financial and personnel management for the school. I will strive for the sustained improvement in the quality of education to help give the students of Laburnum School the best possible opportunity for success.'

And on…

'I will provide a strong, clear voice for all stakeholders and will work to secure commitment of the wider community by developing and maintaining effective networks. I will motivate staff, develop powerful teams, communicate to all stakeholders in a clear and unambiguous fashion, and encourage creativity of thought to engender a positive learning environment.'

Part way into this dirge I start to lose the will to breathe and, as a distraction, begin to doodle in my note pad. Although my backside stings like mad the pain is, nothing compared to the irritation encouraged by the monotony of her voice and the putrid prose, which she has penned to assault our ears. At the end of the monotonous monologue, the three lap dogs decide to show their appreciation by offering a spontaneous round of applause whilst Shirley remains unmoved and I continue to doodle.

Once upon a time I had aspirations of being an artist and do not lack a certain graphic skill with pen or pencil. The dragon I am sketching begins to resemble the inhabitant of my dreams; its evil mouth dripping with acid saliva, its nostrils venting flame and its great scaly wings outspread. The drawing totally immerses me and I am oblivious to all around me. I hear noises, but it takes several moments to realise it is someone talking to me; it is the dragon and she is not happy.

'What are you doing?' she snaps.

I lay more scales on its voluminous body, shading half of each facet giving a three-dimensional feel to the creature.

'I asked you, what are you doing?' she persists.

I smile down at the dragon. I am its creator, its master and her questions are of no importance; all that matters is to finish the drawing.

A swift sharp elbow in my ribs from Shirley brings me back to the leadership meeting. I realise everyone around the table is staring at me, but only one is speaking.

'Have you heard a word I've said, Mr Pike?'

Although she hopes to catch me being lax in my attentiveness, she does not realise I have always been excellent at bluffing my way through just such situations as this.

'Every word,' I lie. 'I thought it was an excellent mission statement and I'm sure all of the stakeholders will be very impressed.'

There were a couple of stifled laughs from around the table whilst Lowbridge lets out an angry and exasperated huff through her flared nostrils.

'We finished talking about the statement over ten minutes ago. Would you like to enlighten us with you views on the current issue?'

I have no idea what she's talking about; not one word of what she was speaking about registered. I try desperately to fabricate some sort of blurb I can use as a smoke screen to hide my lack of concentration, but to no avail. I am lost at sea, floundering on an ocean of uncertainty and ignorance.

The battleship HMS Lowbridge decides to fire all torpedoes and sink any hope I have of remaining afloat.

'We'll take a comfort break here, if you don't mind,' she tells everyone. 'I need to talk to Mr Pike privately for a few minutes; we'll reconvene at half-past.'

The others in the room quickly scuttle out like so many zebra relieved in the knowledge the lion has its claws in another unsuspecting member of their herd.

She makes certain the door has closed before she turns to fix her predator-like eyes on me.

'I'm going to warn you now,' she begins. 'It's the only warning you will get, so if I were you I would pay attention.'

I look her straight in the eyes unable to offer any form of comment. Again, in her company, I find I am a rabbit, transfixed by the glare of the juggernaut's headlights. My mind offers the speculation that she may hold some mystical power over me; she may be able to petrify my very vocal chords each time she confronts me.

'The next time you decide to ignore what is being said in a meeting,' she says as she casually reaches over to take my notebook and study the sketch I had been working on, 'I will have to regard it a lack of professionalism and a failure to carry out your duties.'

With total disdain, she slowly tears the page containing my dragon rendering from my notebook, rips the sheet in to several small pieces and screws them into a ball.

'I would be left with little choice other than to initiate a complete review of your capacity to cope with the rigours of school leadership. In effect I would be asking if you have the ability to do your job.'

As she says this, she stands up and awkwardly stretches over the meeting room table to throw the paper ball in the waste paper bin.

Instantly the image of her, bent over the table in front of me on the patio under the sunshade of our villa, flashes into my mind.

'C'mon man, do your duty! I haven't got all day.'

I stare down at the two great mounds of bloated, puckered flesh waiting for me.

'No, I can't do it!' I declare involuntarily.

'I beg your pardon?' she asks, 'Did I hear you correctly?'

'Hear what?' I offer as my only form of defence, still somewhat dazed by the cruel image dwelling in my brain.

'Did you refuse to comply?'

'No,' I reply, thinking of her threat. 'Yes,' I say remembering her hideous buttocks.

'I'll be honest with you Mr Pike, your colleague, Ken Grayman, has already warned me about your inability to concentrate on your work.'

Ken Grayman? Wait until I get the opportunity to see that double crossing little pot-bellied shit alone. He's always been a devious and conniving closet Judas. Now he has someone to give ear to his whining so that he can spread his own particular brand of venom. She, it appears, is all too receptive to that type of person. I will need to be careful.

'You've heard what I have to say. It's now up to you,' she concludes. 'I hope I will have your attention for the rest of the meeting.'

I drive home later to an empty house. I decide to go and sit outside in the back garden and take in the pleasant late summer evening. I sit on a bench staring out at the immaculately kept garden with the wonderful array of stunning rose bushes and realise how much I miss my wife. I feel tears running down my face. I want her back, but have no idea how to make it happen. She flatly refuses to communicate with me and has already instructed her solicitor to start divorce proceedings. All at once, I feel hopeless at work and helpless in life. Aimlessly I reach out and pluck a rose-head from the nearest bush; it is in its last stage of bloom and showing signs of withering at the edges. I study the beauty of each perfectly formed petal, the intricate pattern of veins on the leaves surrounding the head and then crush the flower in my clenched fist. I feel the sap and juice from the bloom run through my fingers before I discard it on the gravel at my feet.

Over the last few months, my life at work and home has been crumbling away. I have been humiliated, intimidated, threatened, slapped and now I face divorce. In every battle, I appear to be inadequate in the task of self-defence but, as everyone would appreciate, you can lose a battle and still survive to fight another day.

'This is war,' I shout, not caring if the neighbours hear me. I go indoors to defrost a pizza and make my plans.

CHAPTER 7

CONCRETE COWS AND THE GARDENER'S LAST CARAVAN

"Power can be taken, but not given. The process of the taking is empowerment in itself."
Gloria Steinem

'All I'm saying is that Kaz Lowbridge told me you would make all the final arrangements.'

Tanya Raymond, Head of art is standing in my new Deputy Headteacher office, though it's an over-exaggeration to call it an office as its proportions have more in common with the average cereal packet.

Immediately after she arrived at the start of the new term Lowbridge started reallocating the spaces the school leaders were allowed to inhabit. My own office space has been reduced by seventy-five percent, whilst hers extended to cathedral proportions. She claimed this was necessary in order to accommodate the number of important meetings she would be hosting in the coming months.

Tanya has been sent to talk to me about another mundane task I have been assigned by Her Ladyship Lowbridge. This has been the way of it for the last few weeks. Mr Pike is the new jobsworth of the school. Send him the crap, send him the rubbish and make his job so bloody tedious the poor bugger will go totally insane; we can then bring into question the matter of his incompetency and his ability to do the job.

'Concrete cows you say?' I ask, still disbelieving the facts of the case that has been presented to me.

'Hermann Grund is a very well respected London based, Austrian sculptor. We are so lucky to have him working in residence for a week,' says Tanya, slightly nonplussed at my less than ecstatic attitude.

'And this Hermann Grund wants to make forty life-sized concrete cows. Why would we want him to do that?'

'Oh, Bob!' she huffs throwing her hands in the air in a barely adequate display of histrionics. 'As I've already explained, the cows are already made and will be delivered next week. Hermann will arrive the week after and it's during that week our kids will decorate the sculptures under his supervision. What Kaz Lowbridge needs you to do is organise the event; the timetabling, the staff required, you know the sorts of things.'

'You want me to make the event work,' I reply, my enthusiasm less than stoked. I take out my pen and begin to write some notes. 'Forty life-sized cows; what breed?'

'What do you mean, what breed? Does it matter?'

'It could make one hell of a difference to their size.'

'Bob, they're cow-sized.'

'As you've said, but some cows are massive, some are small, some are fat and some are lean,' I reply, inwardly

65

thinking that some even sit in great palatial offices on their voluminous backsides giving out orders whilst I'm cooped up in this shoe box sorting out crap like this!'

'When the project is over we will have lots of great sculptures to put around the school. This is such an exciting opportunity for the art department.'

'Moooooo!' I reply.

At present, my life in this school is the working equivalent of being a crap collector at Newmarket. This is all due to Lowbridge and her vindictive nature. Last week, for example, Her Ladyship called me to her office and instantly demanded to know why there was an old caravan in one corner of the school playing fields.

As part of what I see to be her obvious strategy to discredit me, any aspect of the school she is dissatisfied with is squarely and firmly deposited on my lap. If I should fail to provide the correct answers or solve the problems she regularly presents me with, she will pounce.

I did, however, know about the caravan...

'That's the gardener's caravan,' I informed her. 'There's been a caravan in that place since the school opened back in the fifties. You would have seen it if you'd looked at the old photographs of the school in the foyer before you had them all removed and the place painted salmon pink.'

'And why does the gardener require a caravan, pray tell me?'

'To live in,' I told her.

'To live in? Why on earth do we require a gardener to live on site?'

'Well, it's a sort of tradition. When the school was built in nineteen fifty-one, Bill's father was offered the job of keeping the grounds and tending the flowerbeds and planters. Bill's father was used to life on the road, but he accepted the position provided he could site his horse drawn caravan on the field. When his father died in seventy-eight Old Bill took over, but the caravan was, by then, falling to pieces and so the school bought Bill a new one; he's lived there ever since.'

'You do realise we're not covered by insurance to have someone sleeping on the fields overnight?'

I could see where she was going with this, but there was no way I could be deemed culpable in this situation.

'It's nothing to do with me. I started at the school nearly fifteen years after Bill inherited the job as gardener.'

'Damn it man, you were the Acting Headteacher for nearly a year. You had time then to sort things out,' she spat, each word laden with utter contempt for me. 'I'm surprised the Education Authority allowed you employ someone on such a basis.'

'He's not actually on the payroll,' I said. 'We pay him each week out of petty cash.'

It's not hard to imagine her reaction and very soon after we were in the finance manager's office.

'Yes we do pay Bill Trundell in cash, but it's paid as an honorarium and not exactly out of petty cash,' said Amanda Porter, the Bursar. Amanda is a very large woman whose main pastime seems to be the consumption of vast quantities of bacon sandwiches and doughnuts.

'How do we sort out his tax and National Insurance?' asked Lowbridge.

'Well, that's the point, isn't it?' replied Mrs Porter, but not before she had filled her mouth with another good helping of fried pig and Hovis. 'The thing is, we don't pay him enough to bother about tax and such. In fact, the gardener's wages have not been raised since the late nineteen seventies, when Old Bill took over from his father.'

As she spoke, I could see tiny chunks of chewed bread and bacon flying from her open mouth and land on various parts of her desk. I expect that when she gets peckish she gathers all the tasty morsels together and reshapes them into another snack before the next plate of jam doughnuts are delivered from the kitchens.

'Oh my God!' cursed Lowbridge. 'How many more laws can we break? Has no one here heard of the minimum hourly rate?'

'Well,' continued the still masticating Bursar. 'I did approach one of the previous Headteachers and suggest that we should make everything official and above board, but he told me not to bother and to leave things as they were.'

'Which previous Headteacher was this?' asked Lowbridge.

'Mr Pike here, about six months ago.'

Even before she spoke the words, I had a good idea of what was coming. Amanda Porter and I had never quite seen eye to eye over the financial organisation of the school. There had been a number of times during my stint as Headteacher where we came to blows over the way in which the school budget was allocated. I had no recollection of discussing the wages of Old Bill the gardener; it is quite possible it had slipped my memory, but she was more likely to be using it as an opportunity to score some points at my expense in the presence of Heap Big Chief Lowbridge.

I realised it would be no use trying to defend myself over this issue as Lowbridge would inevitably take the ammunition provided and use it against me at some time yet to come. All I could hope to do was roll with the blow and do the best I could to recover.

She waited until we were back in her office before she began her war dance.

'This is sheer incompetence on your behalf, you realise?' she said, as she sat smugly behind her glass-topped desk on her new black leather Captain's chair. 'You will have to sort this out. You will go and see this Bill personage and tell him his wages will be raised, but that he will need to start paying National Insurance and tax. You will also inform him that he will no longer be able to live on this site in the caravan. You should advise him to apply for council accommodation. There will be no more caravans provided for gardeners on my watch.'

'I'll do my best,' I reply, 'but he probably won't listen. Bill is a proud old man and only takes orders from the Headteacher.'

'Very well,' she said, 'fetch him here and I'll speak to him, but I still hold you responsible for this mess and I want you at the meeting with him.'

This is what I had hoped for. Let her deal with Old Bill and perhaps she wouldn't be so keen to delve too deeply into some of the other traditions of Laburnum High. Best of all, she had offered me a ringside seat for the encounter with Old Bill; this could be a decision she would live to regret.

A little later, I asked Tom Lavender, the site manager and the person closest to Old Bill, to deliver the message indicating the gardener should attend a meeting with the Headteacher later that day. Now, with all the seeds sown, I could sit back and wait for the fun to start.

I met Bill outside Lowbridge's office at the appointed time. I had always had a soft spot for the old man and he was always pleased to see me. He is a fantastic gardener and when he found out my wife Valerie was a keen practitioner in the art of cultivating roses he regularly gave me cuttings and seeds to take home.

As usual, Old Bill looked terribly nervous and jumpy. He did not often enter the school building. During my time at the school I had only known him enter the main block once before, and that was to complain about some vandalism to one of his planters. To be honest, the kids at the school very rarely went near the planted beds or the many pots, planters and window boxes. This was not necessarily out of respect for Bill, but more out of fear of Bill, for whilst nervous inside buildings he shows no lack of courage in protecting his prized displays.

We entered the room together and were faced by Lowbridge, posed behind her desk with her reading glasses perched on the end of her nose, scrutinising a document. At that very moment I realised she bore an uncanny resemblance to Jeremy Paxman.

'Ms Paxman, sorry I mean Ms Lowbridge, may I introduce you to Old Bill Trundell, our gardener and the longest serving member of staff at Laburnum School,' I began then turned to the old man. 'Bill, this is Ms Katherine Lowbridge, the new Headteacher.'

She looked up from the document and peered over the top of her spectacles to regard the old man, standing before her wringing his cap.

'Ah, Mr Trundell, come in and take a seat.'

Even though she tried to appear friendly and at ease with the old man, she could not disguise the distaste she had for his appearance.

Bill lived almost like a hermit. His clothes were filthy, as was he. He gave off a very strong, pungent, toe curling body odour. It must have been difficult for her to allow him into her inner sanctum, let alone to sit on one of her new expensive chairs next to her prized designer desk.

Bill stayed rooted to the spot, just inside her room. She interpreted his body language as fear, another drastic miscalculation, and she set about in her own unique condescending way to try and make him feel more comfortable. 'Don't be frightened.' she said. 'I just want to talk to you and ask you a few questions.'

Bill shuffled forward, staring at her all the time; he remained standing.

'I can understand that it may be slightly intimidating meeting me here, but I assure you I only want to talk about your work at the school,' she continued and held out a hand indicating he should sit on the chair opposite the desk.

He remained upright, his gaze fixed squarely on her.

Awkward silence followed and she became agitated.

'Very well, if you want to stand,' she went on, 'perhaps we can discuss your work. Tell me...'

'Is it a fuckin' woman?' asked Bill as he turned to me, interrupting and totally ignoring her question.

I nodded; it was all I needed to do. He would do the rest.

'I thought I talk with Headmaster, not a fuckin' woman! I hate women. 'Em bad and me hates 'em.'

If I could have photographed the shock that swept across Lowbridge's face I would have had a thousand prints made and scattered them to the four corners of the Education Authority. Now, probably for the first time in her life, she was going to have to cope with a situation that she was not capable of dealing with.

'Fuckers. Cause lots o' problems they do,' he continued, still talking directly to me. 'Hates 'em do I, fuckers. Me Old Da' told me 'bout 'em. Told me not trust 'em. Said they only want get your John Thomas in 'em, then they fucks off and leaves you with a bab to bring up. He hated 'em,' he ranted, then stopped as a thought struck him. 'Your missus, not same as 'em. She likes the blooms, the roses. I like your missus, though I don't want meet 'er. This fucker can't be Headmaster. Headmaster must be good bloke like you an' me. You nice young fella, Mr Pike. You good Headmaster. This one, not even look like woman. I fuckin' hate 'em. Good day, Mr Pike. Hope you Headmaster again soon.'

With that, Old Bill promptly walked out of the room and went back to his duties.

Back in my own tiny excuse for an office, I could not help the feeling of satisfaction as I recalled the way she had squirmed and writhed in Old Bill's presence. Seeing that great bully embarrassed and humiliated was worth its weight in gold. Maybe now she might think before enforcing her will on Laburnum High School and maybe just maybe she had learned an important lesson in how to go about dealing with people.

This state of euphoria induced by witnessing a bully of her magnitude so out of her depth only lasted, however, until Tanya Raymond arrived to inform me I was to organise the artist in residence project. Unhappy as I am at being directed to tackle yet another mind-blowingly tedious task, it was nothing compared to the effect of Tanya's next comment.

'She says you'd be able to accommodate Hermann at your house for the week he's up here from London. She said it would save on hotel costs and that you wouldn't find it an inconvenience at the moment because you have lots of extra space at home.'
'Extra space?' I responded, slightly too aggressively. 'Why would I let some hairy-arsed German hippy stay with me?'
'Keep your hair on, Bob,' she replies, obviously shocked by my outburst. 'Don't shoot the messenger; this is what Kaz told me to say. Besides, he's not German; he's Austrian, although he does look like a hippy.'

I'm outside Lowbridge's office within minutes, knocking on the door and waiting impatiently for her customary "Come in" allowing me entrance. As soon as I hear her voice, I'm through the door and ready to confront her.
'What's the meaning of sending Tanya Raymond to tell me you expect me to house this Austrian sculptor for a week?'

Since her earlier comeuppance at the hands of Old Bill, she has recovered her composure and is once more in pose, scanning a document with spectacles at the end of her nose.

'I merely suggested that since your wife walked out you have plenty of space at your house. It would seem logical to save the school some money by accommodating him. It is only for four nights, after all.'

How the hell does she know that? I've told nobody about Val at school and only my closest friends at the golf club actually know anything about my situation. I decide to challenge her, but she cuts across me.

'Before you start demanding how I happen to know about your home situation, I think you should take a look at this,' she says as she hands me a small card.

I study the card, disbelieving what I'm actually seeing; a membership card to my golf club with her name emblazoned across it.

'I joined two weeks ago and I must say it doesn't take long to get the gossip on other members.'

The gloating, self-glorifying smirk etched on her vulture-like features makes me want to vomit and maybe I should, all over her bloody designer desk and chairs and all over her.

'It would be unfortunate if others in the school community found out about your penchant for exposing yourself in public and your indiscretions with certain Andalucian nymphet's. Hardly the sort of character traits one would expect from a Deputy Headteacher, don't you think?'

The bitch has threatened me again and this time there's nothing I can do. This time she could ruin me if she so wished.

'You'll accommodate Herr Grund and you'll do it willingly. Is that understood?'

Again, the gut-churning smile slides across her evil lips. Defeated, I retreat to the safety of my cornflake packet to lick my wounds.

That night, alone in bed, I feel I am once more without help. My wife is in the process of leaving me and my greatest nemesis now knows secrets about my personal life that could, if she so desired, cripple my career. On top of all this, I must look forward to spending a week cohabiting with some Teutonic tosser from the Tyrol.

Sleep eventually overcomes me and, unsurprisingly, I start to dream.

I am, again, outside the school buildings, but this time there is no dragon to confront me. Instead, a far more frightening creature, Lowbridge herself, faces me.

She sits on the school wall, perched like some huge vulture and as I study her, I see she is covered in feathers of the deepest black. Around her neck she wears, a white ruff of feathers and in place of her nose there sits a huge yellow beak. Like some die-hard birdwatcher I creep closer to the strange beast; she seems unaware of my presence. As I get to within an arm's reach of her she sees me and lets out a fearful squawk.

'Waaaaaaaaaaa! Stop him. Get him. Get him!'

From every window and every doorway, from behind every bike shed and every dustbin come hundreds of concrete cows, all richly decorated. They move towards me in an unrelenting robotic advance. It is not long before I am surrounded and the cattle begin to press against my body; I am slowly being crushed to death. From nowhere comes a streak of light flashing across the sky. The beam shoots towards me then, as it gets close, stops and magically transforms itself into Old Bill, the gardener. He is dressed in an extremely tight fitting blue outfit, complete with red cape and boots. On his chest is emblazoned a large yellow O and B, entwined to form an attractive and intricate logo.

'Have no fear, Headmaster, Old Bill will save you from this fate,' he says and then, with the strength of thousands, begins demolishing the concrete herd.

At last only one of the cows remain and Bill swoops down and plucks it into the air as if it were as light as a feather and hurls it at the huge vulture as she tries to flap her wings and make an escape to the skies above. Unfortunately, for her, Superbill's aim is far too good and the great concrete sculpture hits its target. There is a mighty explosion and when the dust settles all that remains of the once great black bird is a fetid pile of blood and offal scattered over the hard surfaced recreational area of the school.

Bill flies down to stand next to me and we shake hands.

'You were always a good friend to me Headmaster. Both my Dad and I thank you for the things you've done. Goodbye.'

With that, he flew into the sky and once more became a beam of light that shot towards the heavens.

CHAPTER 8

FOUR WHEELBARROWS AND A FUNERAL

"Your hands so skilled and tender
That nurtured so many seeds to grow
Are now returned to dust themselves
As in the soil you go."
Koyleey Bennett - Year 8 pupil, Laburnum School

The death of Old Bill Trundell was a shock to only a few of us at Laburnum High School as not all staff even knew of his existence. To the pupils he was just part of the furniture; like an old desk, here one day and gone the next. In life, he kept himself to himself and got on with his work. The only time he was seen around was when a flower bed or a planter was damaged, or when he was out cutting the grass on the school playing fields or when he made one of his regular visits to the local shops or the post office.

He died as he had lived, alone in his little caravan. Like so many great artists, his true gift to society was only truly acknowledged once he had thrown off his mortal coils. People soon began talking about how he would be missed and how wonderfully vibrant and colourful the school looked. Shortly after his death was announced pupils, parents and staff began to demand some sort of monument to his long service and the contribution he had made to Laburnum High School.

Lowbridge hardly passed comment on the matter. However, the day after his body had been found she did send me instruction to clear the caravan and have it removed from the site immediately.

Therefore, it is, with a heavy heart, I now find myself in Old Bill's caravan sorting through his personal belongings. They found him lying on his bed and later the doctors said he had died of a heart attack.

I move through the caravan looking through the myriad of boxes he had accumulated. In each box there are copies of old gardening magazines, reams of typed articles and an abundance of seed catalogues. On the small rickety kitchen table sits an old typewriter with a pile of white dog-eared paper next to it.

On the wall in his bedroom hangs a framed black and white signed photograph of Percy Thrower with the inscription: "To William. Don't believe a word of it! Best wishes, Percy T". Next to this is another photograph, this time in colour, of Alan Titchmarsh. The inscription reads: "Thanks Bill (Mister Rose). I owe it all to you."

I would like to stop and ponder the import of these cryptic comments from the pair of green-fingered superstars, but something else in the bedroom has caught my eye.

Next to the bed, on a small cluttered shelf strewn with seed packets, small seed pots and a rusty dibber, sits another photograph in a small silver frame on top of a folded piece of paper. The picture shows Bill as a lad of about fifteen, with his Dad, standing in front of the school gates. Behind them hangs a banner displaying the words "Grand opening of Laburnum School 1951" clearly visible. It is not the photograph, however, which interests me, but the folded paper beneath it.

Now unfolded, I can see it is school headed notepaper with the signature indicating that it is from Katherine Lowbridge.

Dear Mr Trundell,

Following our recent meeting, in which you demonstrated behaviour that I found deeply offensive, I have had no alternative but to refer the matter to the Governors.

Having considered the incident they have asked me to inform you that your services will no longer be required by the school and that you will need to leave the premises and vacate the caravan situated on the school grounds no later than a week from the date of this communication.

I understand you may wish to appeal against this decision, but I must point out that as you are employed on a casual basis and not on the official payroll of the school, your rights in this matter are severely limited.

The Governors have asked me to express their sincere gratitude for the service you have given to the school over the years.

Yours faithfully

Katherine N. Lowbridge

The letter is dated yesterday; the day he died. At the side of the bed is the envelope printed with his name and marked "Private and Confidential" in the top right-hand corner. Having read the letter here, on his bed, the shock of knowing he was going to lose not only his livelihood but also his home must have been too much for Old Bill. His heart couldn't take it and he died here. She killed him. She killed him as sure as anything!

I've had enough. I storm out of the caravan and steer a direct course across the playing fields towards the main building and her office. This disrupts the year 10 football match taking place and I'm aware of a certain amount of abuse being thrown my way but I continue to march on determinedly, on course for a showdown with Lowbridge.

'Mr Pike,' calls out Tom Lavender, as he intercepts me near the long-jump pit. 'I hoped I'd catch you before the end of the day.'

'Sorry Tom, but I'm in the middle of something important,' I say as I try to step past him, but he, too, is determined in his mission. 'This won't take long, Bob; it's about Old Bill.'

Now I stop and listen. He has my attention; what other ammunition might there be for me to use against her?

'Okay Tom, I'm listening,' I reply, thankful I am not downwind of him.

'Well it's like this. A few months ago … well it could have been a few years ago … no, no it was last year, Old Bill and me were talking and he says to me, "when I die will you scatter my ashes on the flower beds of the school?"

'Yes, yes, Tom, get to the point,' I say, impatient for my conflict with Lowbridge to begin.

'Well, I was wondering if the school would see fit in granting me and a few others permission to have a little memorial ceremony after his cremation when we can lay him to rest with his flowers and his prized roses.'

'Yes, of course we can.' I make the decision on impulse and without consulting Lowbridge.

'Good, then me and some of the other staff thought you should be invited to be one of the people to scatter the ashes, if that's ok? Old Bill was very fond of you. '

'Yes,' I say. 'That would be fine.'

As I speak, I notice something happening on the playing field at the opposite end to Old Bill's caravan.

'What the hell is that thing, Tom?' I ask him, changing the topic of our conversation completely.

I'm referring to a huge, timber-made framework rising some twenty feet above the grass of the field.

'Oh that's Mr Forrest's tree bucket, or whatever the flippin' thing is called. Him and the kids work on it after school. He's told me what it will do, but between you and me I think he's a nutcase and that the thing will fall down sooner than throw a Mini the length of the field.'

'Throw a what?' I ask, still not quite believing my own ears.

'Throw a Mini-car over four-hundred metres. He says it will be a world record and that means the school will get its name in The Guinness Book of Records. He's off his rocker.'

Satisfied he has got the answer he wanted regarding the disposal of the old gardener's remains, Tom Lavender trudges off to get on with his work, which probably entails filling in another batch of contractor requisition forms.

I stroll over to the massive siege engine being constructed to a scale the presentation had failed to do justice. Could this thing really do what Derek Forrest is claiming? Was he really intending to throw a Mini the length of the field? My mind flashes back to the scene of devastation on my drive and the small green Mini Cooper, wrecked to almost "write off" proportions.

'I hope he's filled in a risk assessment for this baby,' I say to myself. 'She'll go bloody mad when she finds out.'

The funeral was intended to be a small affair. However, once news of Old Bill's funeral spread many parents, former pupils, the manager of the local garden centre, two town Councillors, an Alderman and a reporter from the local press attended. In addition, the School Council insisted on sending ten representatives to pay their respects and those teachers and ancillary staff who were not with classes chose to attend. In total sixty-five people went to the crematorium.

I organised the school minibus to transport the kids whilst myself and Tom Lavender provided transport for other staff. Not surprisingly, there was a dash for my car in preference for Tom's when the time came to leave the school, and not only because mine is a big BMW.

Lowbridge, as befits her nature, declined to attend "due to a pressing engagement" and proclaimed that I should be her representative. Her absence did not go down well with the parents, children, staff or dignitaries.

It was four in the afternoon and school was over for the day when everybody arrived back on site for the ceremony of scattering Old Bill's ashes; even some of the parents and officials came, as did the reporter.

Tom Lavender had provided four bright, new wheelbarrows full of compost to form the lead in the procession to the site where Old Bill's ashes would be scattered. He asked me if I would push the lead barrow; a task I happily accepted.

So I find myself at the head of a column of nearly thirty people all solemnly making their way across the playing field to the flower beds where Old Bill will finally be laid to rest.

As we make the slow progress to our destination, I can't help looking over to the hard-surfaced recreation area and notice that it is occupied by a herd of cattle, but not just any cattle; these are concrete cattle, freshly arrived from the funny farm.

'Do you see Bill? It seems like everyone's turned out for you,' I whisper.

We arrive at the beds and Tom takes out a piece of paper from his jacket pocket. He begins to read.

'Well Bill, you cared for these beds all your life, just as your Dad did all his. Now it's time for you to have a good rest and sleep with the flowers and plants you so loved.'

Tom takes the urn from Thelma Burton, the head cleaner, who has carried it carefully during the procession. He opens the lid and scatters a portion of the ashes into each of the wheelbarrows.

'Now gentlemen, would you spread the contents of your barrows on each of the four beds.'

Obediently, I pour my mixture of ashes and compost onto the nearest bed and I'm handed a rake by a member of the school council so that I can spread out the mixture.

As soon as he's emptied the content of his barrow, Tom takes out his piece of paper once more.

'We've done what you wanted Bill. Now there's one thing you can do for us,' he pauses as his voice cracks; a tear clearly visible in the corner of each eye.

He takes a few seconds to regain his composure before he finishes his speech.

'If you find any weeds down there, give 'em hell!' he finally says and everyone in attendance applauds.

Once the ceremony is concluded people begin making their way back across the field.

'Mr Pike, can I have a word?' asks the reporter from the local rag, as I head back towards the main block of buildings.

'No problem,' I reply. 'What do you want to know?'

'Were you aware that Bill Trundell was one of the country's leading horticulturalists?'

He stops me dead in my tracks.

'You're mad,' I reply. 'Why, Old Bill hardly ever left the site apart from going to the local shops or the post office.'

'He was an authority in many fields, but rose cultivation and cross-breeding in particular. To the gardening world he was known as Mister Rose, but he never sought recognition and fame. He could have been a superstar of the gardening world; instead he communicated with many leading figures purely by mail.'

'The post office!' The words just shoot out. 'He went there three or four times a week, so Tom tells me.'

'You've had a celebrity die on your site, Mr Pike, and you didn't realise it,' he says smugly. 'I'm the first, but I won't be the last reporter you'll have around here once the news spreads.'

I'm speechless.

'There's something else,' he continues. 'Did you see that big black Merc with the darkened windows at the crematorium?'

'Yes I did, as a matter of fact. Why?'

'Do you know who was inside it?'

'No I don't. Why would I?'

'Did you see the number plate?'

'No,' I say, intrigued and irritated at the same time.

'A T 1.'

'What?'

'Alan Titchmarsh.'

CHAPTER 9

NIGHTS IN WHITE SATIN AND THE VIKING QUEEN

"There is nothing safe about sex. There never will be.
Norman Mailer

'You spoke to the press without my consent?'

This is the opening salvo of Lowbridge's now familiar daily rant at me. She's obviously read the interview I gave to the press about Old Bill Trundell and his more renowned alias of Mister Rose.

'You've made me out to be some sort of idiot,' she blasts, standing behind her designer desk frantically waving her arms about. She is coming close to being hysterical. Perhaps, if I push her a little harder, I might get her to reveal her true self. 'You told them that you were the only member of staff to be aware of his other life, that only you knew this "Mister Rose" was his alter-ego.'

'Well that was true,' I answer, even though it wasn't.

'That makes me out to be a fool. It suggests that I do not know my own staff!'

'That's your interpretation,' I say, trying to needle her even more than I already have. 'Am I being instructed to lie on your behalf? Is that what you want me to do for you in future?'

'I want you to be professional in the way you represent this school.'

'And lie?'

'Don't push me too far Pike, or I'll break you.' she screams, her voice on the verge of an uncharacteristic shrillness. 'I have a considerable file on you already. This disregard for my authority could be the straw that breaks the camel's back. I may well go to the Governors and ask to have you suspended while an investigation is carried out into your ability to satisfactorily perform your duties.'

The claws are out; I've done it! As I expected, she's going through the whole bullying routine yet again; first the intimidation, then the soul searching, then the final body blow. This time I'm ready for her; this time I'm going to watch her squirm.

'I also notice that you haven't had that caravan removed from the site yet. That's another task you've failed to carry out and...'

'The caravan is staying where it is.'

There's a priceless pause as she stares at me, wide-eyed. The look on her face says it all; she cannot believe the words I have just uttered.

'What did you say to me?'

'Old Bill's caravan is staying where it is. I want it there for when the national press and the TV companies arrive. No one will move it because there are many, including myself, who would like to see it given the status of a monument to Old Bill and Mister Rose. This is my decision and you will agree with it. Have I made myself clear?'

Astounded, she flops back into her black leather chair, picks up her reading glasses and perches them on the end of her nose. She then reaches for a pen from the desk and starts to write in her notebook.

'Now you've gone too far Pike,' she says, her voice trembling with rage. 'I'm going to suspend you as of this minute and...'

'No, you'll do no such thing,' I respond, as I remove a sheet of folded paper from my pocket and expertly skim it across her desk so that it stops in front of her. 'I'd read that before you do anything else; it's a copy, I have the original.'

She unfolds the paper and begins to scan the words printed on it. It's a photocopy of the letter she sent to Old Bill on the morning of his death.

'He was an old man, working for the love of it and accepting only a few measly pounds in return. He was also a legend amongst the gardening fraternity and you killed him.'

'I didn't know...'

'I told you, but you ignored the fact.'

'You'd lie?'

'I have been known to, when deemed necessary.'

'He was a sexist pig and he broke every rule in school policy.'

'I always found him quite charming,' I reply.

'But you heard him; the way he spoke to me, the things he said.'

'I heard nothing apart from you bullying a harmless old man. You threatened him with eviction and the loss of the only work he ever wanted to do. He left this office a broken man, but you couldn't stop there; you had to see him suffer more, so you sent him that letter with some jumped-up concocted allegations. That's what killed him and that's what the press will hear if you try to suspend me. Just imagine the publicity for the school? Just imagine the publicity for you?'

Casually I walk over to one of her filing cabinets in the corner of the office. I slide the top drawer open and flick through the contents until I find the file I need. It's a thick file with my name printed on it.

'Linda always files the competency folders in the top drawer, but I think the best place for this is here.'

I drop the contents into the waste paper bin and then return the empty folder to the top drawer.

'Will there be anything else?' I ask her, but she is silent.

I exit her office; safe in the knowledge I have defeated her in this battle. I know there are still many fights to come but, for now, I hold the high ground.

In triumphant mood I steer the big BMW on its familiar route home. I approach the drive with extreme caution; a wise move as parked on the drive is an old, uniquely painted, VW camper van.

I pull up close to the van, get out of the car and look at the strange paintwork. The whole of the vehicle has been hand painted with weird ethnic symbols and patterns. In between these graphic renderings, the word LOVE has been painted hundreds of times in hundreds of different styles and colours. I'm still staring, fascinated by the strange multi-coloured old vehicle and wondering to whom it might belong, when I hear a movement behind me. I turn around and come face to face with a giant.

He stands about six feet seven, at least. His blonde hair is very long and gathered in a ponytail. His beard, the same colour as his hair, is also long, but this has been plaited into several braids. He wears faded blue denim jeans and a white t-shirt with the word LOVE emblazoned across his chest. On his feet, he wears a pair of well-used sandals.

'Hi, are you Bob Pike?' says the giant with a slight Germanic accent.

For all the world he looks like an archetypal Viking warrior turned Greenham Common protestor.

'I'm Pike, how can I help you?'

'Pleased to meet you, boss,' he replies and holds out a huge hand to shake mine. 'Hermann Grund, I've been working with your kids today. I'm told I'm bunking here with you tonight.'

'Ah, Mr Grund. Yes. Forgive me, I'd completely forgotten you were here tonight, but don't worry. Grab your things and come in.'

My good mood obviously puts the big Austrian artist at ease and he is soon relaxing with a cup of coffee and talking enthusiastically about his day with the pupils. For my part, I am so grateful for the company I decide to invite the young man for a meal.

'Do you prefer Indian or Chinese?'

'Either's fine by me, Bob.'

The young man is fabulous company and the impromptu evening out turns out to be a delightful success.

Back at the house after the good meal and a few beers we sit talking more about a variety of subjects from art to the cinema, from sport to politics and from trains to tattoo's. We chat hours until tiredness begins to take its toll and encourages me to seek the comfort of my bed.

'Well Hermann, I've had a fantastic night, but I'm worn out. I think it's time I turned in.'

'Ya me too, boss; got a long hard day ahead tomorrow.'

We climb the stairs and I show him his room and the bathroom then I head for my room. I get undressed and check out the scars on my backside. They're still not completely healed, but the pain is nowhere near as bad.

I slip on a bathrobe and look to see if the bathroom is free. The door is ajar so I nip down the corridor to do my evening ablutions. I walk straight in to the bathroom and look at myself in the mirror on the wall opposite, above the washbasin. Still looking into the mirror, I pick up my tooth brush and tube of toothpaste. I'm about to squeeze the stuff out when I notice movement to my right.

'Hi Bob,' says Hermann, towelling himself dry. 'Just had a quick shower. Boy, it was good to get out of those clothes.'

Casually he throws the towel over his shoulder, revealing his full nakedness. He has an impressive physique, on a par with the classic Greek marble statues he so admires. However, it is not his toned muscular frame that gains the focus of my attention; it is the gigantic appendage dangling between his legs.

The realisation that I'm in my bathroom staring at the groin of a naked Austrian sculptor suddenly dawns on me and instantly panic sets in; I babble all sorts of apologies and scurry off to the sanctuary of my room. My heart is thumping and I'm sweating profusely. That was close, but close to what? I begin to calm down and realise nothing happened and that it was just my stupid English male sensibilities kicking in. I've seen men naked before in showers and changing rooms at the gym and the club, so why should I become frantic now? Perhaps it's because it was in my own bathroom, or perhaps, I smile to myself, I was just worried in case Val walked in on us.

With that thought in mind I climb into bed and turn off the lights. My eyes have become heavy with sleep and I am transported to the land of dreams and subconscious fantasy.

I'm lying on a pure white silk sheet in the middle of a multicolored flowerbed. The bloom of each plant sings sweet music and, as I look closer, I see that the head of each flower is that of Old Bill. The song this thousand-headed choir sings is intoxicating in its beauty and fills me with such joy that laughter erupts; I am so happy, so content, so at one with the world.

I see a figure moving towards me through the bushes; it is little Juanita dressed in a diaphanous robe of pure white fabric.

As she skips and dances I notice her perfectly formed breasts bouncing delightfully in time with her movements. She lies at my side on the silk sheet and kisses me with great passion and then she holds the stalk of a nearby plant and begins to squeeze gently. After a few moments sweet fragrant oil erupts from the head of the plant, and runs down the stem over her soft golden hands. Tenderly she gathers the oil and starts massaging my scarred buttocks. The feeling is unbelievable; the softness of her hands and the cool perfumed oil make my pulse quicken and my juices stir. I lie and let the flood of ecstasy consume my body as Juanita skillfully teases and tantalises.

When my orgasm arrives it overwhelms me and I feel every muscle in my body spasm then relax as I spill my seed over the white silk. Juanita brings her delicious lips close to my ear and whispers her love for me. I reply shouting, "I love you my darling!" ten or twenty times as she continues to massage my buttocks. She takes more oil from the flowers and works it into my skin. I feel her sensual finger explore secret places. I've never experienced such pleasure.

I open my eyes. I'm still in bed. I can feel Juanita oiling my buttocks. I turn my head to catch a glimpse of her lovely face. She is lying there smiling at me; my beautiful Juanita. She has grown bigger, I notice, much bigger and her jet-black hair has turned to yellow blonde, tied in a ponytail; she also has a blonde beard.

'Oh my God, Hermann no!' I scream in the manner of a hysteric banshee, either from fear, pain, or shame. Whatever the case I am far too late to affect proceedings and stop the inevitable.

'How was Hermann last night, Bob?' asks Tanya Raymond, plonking herself down in the chair opposite the desk in my office.

'Oh fine,' I reply, while the memory of the agony or the agony of the memory sear through my mind and threaten to remain for many years to come. 'Yeah, we got on well.'

'That's good to hear,' she says, ' but I'm afraid he won't be staying with you again this week.'

'Oh, why not?' I ask, praying that he has not informed others of what transpired.

'He hopes you won't be offended, but he's just found out about Old Bill's caravan and was wondering if he could sleep there for the rest of the week. He says the place has good vibes and that he'd like to do some work on it to help turn it into a fitting monument to the old fella. You aren't unhappy with that are you?'

'No, no, I think it's a fabulous idea and I wouldn't want to miss the opportunity of having such a renowned artist contribute to the memorial for Mister Rose.'

'Thanks Bob. I knew you'd understand. I'll let Hermann know.'

She leaves and I let out one of the biggest sighs of relief you can imagine, then I make a quick mental note never to accept lodgers ever again.

The phone in my office rings. The receptionist tells me she has my wife on the line, so I tell her to put Val through. I'm pleased to hear her voice again and happy to be able to speak to her.

'Hello Val, how are things?' I say, trying to be as buoyant and positive as possible.

'I need to talk to you, Bob. Can we meet on Saturday night? I thought we might book a table at Romero's in town.'

Of course, I agree to the request and we finalise the details of where to meet and at what time. The thought of seeing her excites me and improves my mood; perhaps the ignominy of the night before will soon evaporate.

CHAPTER 10

MEETINGS, MEETINGS, MORE MEETINGS AND ACRONYMS

"People who enjoy meetings should not be in charge of anything."
Thomas Sowell

The one thing I can guarantee you'll learn from a gathering of teachers is... nothing, absolutely zilch, zero, nada.

Staff meetings are generally used as a means for passing on information. The thing I have discovered, having attended countless numbers of these congregations, is that no one listens or pays attention to anything that's said. When I started teaching, years ago, staff meetings took place about once every half term. Departments had informal chats over lunch or when they felt like it. Staff rooms were full at break times and lunchtime. In those days, staff talked to each other rather than listen to pontificating senior leaders (who were not called senior leaders; it was the Head or nothing). Did I feel uninformed? No, and I had time to get on with the job of teaching without feeling frazzled.

Now however, in spite of the Workforce Agreement, the trend is for more meetings. In some schools, as is the case in Laburnum High School, under its new regime, staff meetings (now called briefings) take place every morning in addition to the once weekly meeting at the end of the day.

At these morning meetings, the Head goes through any notices she has and then we go down through the hierarchical pecking order where she asks if any of the leadership team have anything to say. The individual members of the Senior Leadership Team (SLT) then pipes up, each attempting to be wittier or sound more knowledgeable that the previous speaker. Serious consequences can befall any member of the team who tries to alter the acknowledged pecking order.

Once the senior team is out of the way she throws the forum open to the rest of the staff. By this time the bleary-eyed throng have about forty-five seconds left before the bell sounds for the start of the morning session and have to talk at a pace equalling that of a Formula One racing car. No wonder is it, then, facts that might well be useful or important slip through the net.

Today I stand next to Lowbridge as she tells the Laburnum workforce about the list of incredibly important meetings she will be attending during the day. I imagine the staff sitting before her can hardly contain their excitement when Ms L informs them she will be talking to a collection of local councillors about the future of education in the city. However, their state of euphoria will be fuelled to such an extent some may be in danger of passing out as she proudly discloses she will be having a working lunch with the members of the Local Authority Library Service.

The baton of responsibility is presented to me.

'I'd just like to thank everyone that contributed to the flowers for Old Bill,' I say; it is my only notice.

Following me is the resident Judas and self-proclaimed school wit, Ken Grayman. He clucks, struts, and tries his best to be the funny man, but it's Wednesday morning and I've seldom seen a teacher smile on the third morning of the week.

After Grayman come the Assistant Heads, the Trainee Head, the Heads of Upper and Lower school and, finally, the Heads of Year. After this Lowbridge asks…

'Are there any other notices?'

Only two members of staff raise their hands, but there's now less than thirty seconds until the bell.

'Hi! Yeah, just like to thank everyone,' says Tanya Raymond, 'that helped with the Artist in Residence project, especially Bob Pike, who arranged all the staffing and put Hermann up for the night.'

I would have preferred not to have been reminded of my encounter with the "giant" Austrian as the memory is still incredibly painful.

Only ten seconds until the bell and Andrea Freeman, Head of languages is on her feet.

'Next Monday we have a Spanish exchange teacher starting at the school for ten weeks and we'd like to know if anyone has a spare room they could use while they're over here,' she shouts as the bell for the start of lessons rings out. 'If you do, can you let me know!'

Her last words are eaten up by the noise created by hordes of stampeding children and the collective groan of seventy plus teachers. I was probably the only one listening to her words and I will certainly not be offering my services.

Back in the confines of my cornflake box, I consult my daily diary in the hope that something interesting may be happening today. Unfortunately, very little of note is on offer apart from the three meetings I have arranged for this afternoon. The first is with Derek Forrest, the second is with young Daniel Webster and the third is with Toby Marriott. My only other appointment for the day is a scheduled meeting with our S.I.P.

Sip, I hate acronyms. The education profession seems obsessed by the things. Why? No group can exist in education without first developing its acronym; no initiative can be successful without a string of catchy linked letters that, together, form some neat little title.

Lowbridge is a prime example of the sort of educationalist who thrives on acronyms. Since her arrival, we have had several task groups, meeting cycles, initiatives and awards established, all with their own unique acronym. We have T.A.G (Teaching Action Group), S.A.M.I.S (Special Award for the Most Improved Student), S.N.O.G. (Student Nominated Operational Group) and H.A.G.S (Headteacher and Governors working with Students). I've even been to a meeting chaired by our illustrious Headteacher where the whole two hours of allotted time was spent deciding on the name and the acronym for the group.

Many of the acronyms we face on a daily basis, are of course, those that come to us via the LA (Local Authority) or central government offices – the DCSF, or is it the

DSCF? Remembering the correct wordings of so many codes can be a nightmare. Still, you always have your S.I.P. to help out if you get stuck.

The S.I.P. is what is known as a School Improvement Partner. These are people who have had special training in understanding acronyms. They come into school on a regular basis to meet with the school leadership and bestow upon us their wisdom in the hope that the school will improve. A S.I.P. will always be an experienced professional, possibly a serving Headteacher or someone recently retired. The premise is that they will have a wealth of knowledge about current educational practice and they will be totally professional. However, as I've found on numerous occasions, what you expect in education seldom turns out to be what you get. That Gilbert Quantock, our own appointed S.I.P, ever managed to become a Headteacher is remarkable in itself; that after he retired anyone should consider him able to help and improve other schools is, quite frankly, insane.

'Hi Bob,' says Gilbert as he enters my S.L.A.Z. (Senior Leader Administration Zone). 'I believe I'm due to see you for an hour now.'

'Yes, Gilbert. Come in,' I reply, as I consult my A.P.A.D. (Automated Period Allocation Device – or 'watch', if you prefer). 'Please take a S.C.A.S.M (Specialised Comfort and Support Mechanism) and sit down.

I offer him a coffee, which he gratefully accepts, and then he sits down and places his attaché case at the side of his chair. Once seated, he looks at me with a big beaming smile on his face.

'Well then, what are we going to talk about?' he asks.

'I believe Ms Lowbridge wants us to talk about last year's examinations and specifically the GCSE results.'

'Yes, that was it. Your results; shocking aren't they?' he replies, still with his inane grin fixed in position. 'Sometimes I wonder why we bother, don't you? We teach them for five bloody years and then the little buggers make a total bollocks of their exams.'

He reaches down to grab his case and takes out a set of papers.

'I've brought some C.A.D.S for you to look at. I think it stands for Comparative Assessment Data Sheets, but don't quote me on it. I can't make any sense of the numbers on them, but you might as well get some use out of the blasted things.'

'Ms Lowbridge suggested I pick your brains for strategies to help improve our results,' I say, hoping he might produce a magic wand or something just as useful.

'Did she? Well, I suppose I am your Improvement Partner, but I'm not a bloody miracle worker. I mean, how an earth are you blokes supposed to teach the sods if half of them are truanting most of the year and those that stay in school cause so much trouble you feel like giving up? I don't know how you younger chaps stick at it these days. At least when I was teaching you could whack the bastards. Nowadays if you so much as breathe near one of them the parents are screaming assault and if you look at one of the little blighters, then you're a bloody pervert!'

He once more reaches into his attaché case again and removes from it a small silver hip flask.

'Don't mind if I have a drop of advisor's ruin…?' he asks as he holds the flask over his coffee waiting for me to give approval to pour.

'No, not at all, Gilbert – go ahead.'

'Do you fancy a snifter, old man?'

'Not for me thanks, I try not to touch the stuff before break time.'

'Really? Oh, I always used to have a couple of stiff snorts of scotch before I took assembly in the morning. It always helped the story of the Good Samaritan fly by.'

He tips a goodly amount into his coffee and then replaces the flask.

'Now, where were we? Oh yes, results. Have you ever thought about cheating?'

'I'm sorry, Gilbert, I don't understand what you mean?'

'Cheating. Giving the kids the answers, or better still doing the exams for them.'

'Isn't that a rather risky strategy?' I ask.

'Only if you get caught; besides, would anyone really care so long as your results improved? The Government wouldn't give a damn, would they? Not if their figures were improved at the same time. Cheat, it's the only way to ensure success.'

'It's not really ethical though, is it?'

'Suppose not, but that's what happens when you have targets and league tables,' he replies and then takes a big swig of his coffee. 'Still, she wanted a strategy and I think that is my best suggestion.'

He takes another gulp of his alcohol-laced beverage.

'She's a formidable looking woman, your Miss Lowbrdge. God, she's big and built like a prop forward, but not as attractive. She must scare the living daylights out of most of the staff. I'm just glad I don't work with her.'

'But Gilbert, I thought that was the whole point. You're our S.I.P and you're supposed to work with her.'

While I'm talking he has taken out the flask once more and is pouring the rest of its contents into the almost empty cup.

'Ah yes,' he says, taking another swig. 'What does "S.I.P" stand for again? Bloody terrifying looking woman though. Wouldn't like to be underneath a tree that she fell out of'

The rest of our meeting passes without as much as one word relating to education. Following his less than flattering comments about Lowbridge, Gilbert talked about the state of English cricket, the quality of fruit and veg since we entered the Common Market and the reasons why he hates Norwegians.

Gilbert Quantock eventually leaves my office wearing his inane grin and taking with him an empty hip flask. He is probably the biggest P.R.A.T. I've ever had the misfortune to meet in education.

The lunch period has just finished and I'm awaiting the arrival the first of my afternoon appointments.

Derek Forrest is, as always, punctual to the second and as ebullient as ever. He walks in proudly carrying a highly detailed scale model of his trebuchet under his arm.

'Here it is, Bob,' he proclaims, as he places the model on the desk right in front of me. 'What do you think of that baby?'

I'm not one bit interested in the toy before me.

'Will the real thing work?'

'Of course it will,' replies Forrest with more than a hint of *I'm offended you even asked* evident in his tone.

'And is it true you hope to get yourself into The Guinness Book of Records by throwing a Mini over four hundred yards?'

'Yes. Well it's actually four hundred metres, but yes, we think we can, so long as we get everything right in the construction.'

I look at the exquisitely made model sitting on my blotter pad and examine each of the small moving parts including the little weight, the catapult arm and the slingshot.

'Will it be accurate?'

Derek Forrest is about to answer, then thinks better of it. Instead, he takes the model and produces a small toy car from his jacket pocket. He places the model at one end of my desk and primes it by placing the toy car in the slingshot. He then takes a small box of paper clips from the desk and positions it on the shelf at the other end of the small room.

'That distance is roughly equivalent to four hundred metres if this were the real thing,' he says as he points at the scale model. 'The key is making certain the machine is primed accurately. One error here and the ammunition could sail off course by many metres.'

He re-checks the setting of the model and, when satisfied, he pulls back a tiny leaver and releases the mechanism. The toy car flies straight as an arrow across the room and right on target, the small box explodes, sending paperclips flying in all directions. Quite simply, I'm amazed.

'I could hit that thing nineteen times out of twenty and the full sized one will be just as accurate,' he states proudly.

'Well, I have to say I'm very impressed. This could be very good publicity for the school and to get into The Guinness Book of Records as well. What more can I say? When do you think you'll be attempting the record?'

'Hopefully we'll be making our first test shots in about four weeks, so I would think we'll be ready for the attempt in six or seven weeks.'

'That's excellent Derek,' I say, massaging his massive ego. 'One other thing, before you go.'

'What's that, Bob?'

'How's young Webster getting on?'

'He's a born leader and, without doubt, my best worker. Apart from me, he probably knows more about the project than any of the others.'

'Oh good, I'm glad we found something to motivate the young man. He's had a rough life and we seem to be offering him something he's never had before.'

'What?' says Forrest looking bemused, 'A chance to build a fully working mediaeval French trebuchet?'

'No Derek. A chance to be part of a team and having a sense of worth.'

Twenty minutes later the boy himself is sitting in front of me. He looks far smarter than when I last saw him.

'I'm hearing good things about your progress, Daniel, and Mr Forrest tells me you're the star of his technology project.'

'Things are okay here,' he replies.

He has new shoes and is wearing a new sweater.

'Have you seen your mum lately?'

'Yeah, they say I'll be back with her by Christmas. Thank you.'

He obviously imagines I've interceded with the authorities and helped speed up his reunion with his mother. I've done no such thing, but it won't do any harm to cultivate this impression.

'I told you I'd help out if I could.'

I delve into my pocket and take out my wallet. I pull three crisp twenty-pound notes from inside and hand them to the boy. He accepts the money without question and stuffs it into his pocket.

'I may ask you to do some small favours for me in the future, Daniel. Mainly information gathering and that sort of thing.'

'No problem,' he replies. 'Just let me know what you want. Do you need to know about staff or kids?'

He's razor sharp and a good ally to have, but now is not the time to use him. For now, it's just important to know he's in my camp.

'I'll tell you when the time comes. In the meantime, keep popping in to see me. I like to know how you are getting on.'

My last appointment of the day, predictably, arrives late. Just as Derek Forrest is a model of punctuality, Toby Marriott is a perfectionist in the art of tardiness. As always, he has an excuse.

'Sorry I'm late, Bob, only I just popped in to see Andrea to offer the use of a room for the new Spanish exchange teacher.'

'Toby, you live in a one bedroom flat; you don't have a spare room.'

'Ooops,' he mocks. 'Still, I've seen some of these Spanish senoritas before. They can be really hot. I think it's because of all the sun they get.'

'Yes I know,' I reply, for an instant transported to that afternoon beneath the shade on the patio with little Juanita.

'So I thought I'd get in there and stake my claim,' he smirks. 'And if she's an ugly old witch then I can say I was mistaken and there ain't no room at the inn.'

'You're a scheming, fornicating, little shit, Toby and one day someone's going to fix you good and proper.'

'Yeah, but at least I will have enjoyed myself before it happens.'

'Well, keep your whimsical little philosophical insights to yourself and listen to me. A while back, I said I would eventually need to call in a favour. Well, that time has arrived.'

Immediately his good humour drops and an extremely worried look appears on his youthful features.

'Oh don't worry. I'm not going to ask you to commit murder. I just want you to collect some information about someone.'

'Who?' he asks, his face full of trepidation and fear.

'I want you to find out as much as you can about Katherine Lowbridge. I literally want to know what makes her tick, especially what she does in her spare time. Find out as much as you can about her.'

'Bob, you're not going to ask me to sleep with her are you?' he almost whimpers.

'Oh, don't flatter yourself, sonny. When I said I'd use you, it wasn't because I thought I could pimp for you. I just need facts, figures, and details. Understand?'

He lets out an audible sigh of relief and at the same time, the terror reflected in his face disappears. He becomes, once more, the exuberant cheeky ladies' man.

'Wow! For one moment I thought you were going to ask me to... you know... with her... No, I couldn't; even I have limits. Why do you want to know this stuff?'

'Mind your own bloody business and don't go letting on to anyone that I've asked you to do this. If you do I'm likely to uncover some more evidence concerning you and a certain pupil; you get my meaning?'

By the look on his face, he certainly does.

CHAPTER 11

DOUBLE VISION AND DOUBLE CROSSES

"Love: a temporary insanity, curable by marriage.
Ambrose Bierce

I arrive at Romero's at seven-thirty on the dot and Val is there ready waiting for me just inside; she always did keep good time. The waiter asks us if we'd like to have a drink in the bar or go straight to the table. We choose the latter option and are soon sitting facing each other. Her face glows radiantly in the candlelight. It's quite obvious she has taken some time getting ready for our engagement; she looks stunning, a real vision. Her tall slender frame displayed to perfection in the gorgeous black evening dress she has chosen to wear and her choice of jewellery, as always, is exemplary.

For the first half hour, whilst we order drinks and select our food, our conversation is polite and undemanding. By the time we start to eat our meal the talk between us has dwindled to the usual comments about the standard of the dishes set before us. Only when coffee arrives does the real reason for our rendezvous raise its head.

'I've spent a lot of time thinking over the past few weeks, Robert,' she begins, using the name she calls me when we have serious matters to discuss, 'and I've come to the conclusion that I've been hard on you.' She has my full and undivided attention.

'When I stopped to analyse it that unfortunate little incident with Monica was actually quite amusing and the crash with the Mini was a pure accident, I'm sure.'

I nod in recognition of her change of heart.

'Then we come to the issue of that little Spanish tart.'

She picks up her wine glass and takes a good swig of the Châteauneuf-du-Pape before continuing to speak.

'I realise you were out there, on your own, lonely and in need of company … in need of female company. I told myself, you're a man with needs and a man with a healthy sexual appetite. I understand what you must've been going through and, even though I can't forget what happened, if you promise me that nothing like that will ever happen again I can forgive you. If you can promise and you want to get back together then I think we should try.'

This is the best news I could possible hope to hear. Since Val left I have been so lonely and have yearned to be with her. How can I do anything but agree?

'I will never, ever disappoint you again, my darling,' I reply as I take her delicate hand in mine and squeeze it tenderly. 'I've missed you so much and could only dream this day would come. When will you move back?'

She takes another long gulp of wine; it's almost as if she's relieved by the outcome.

'Within the week, as soon as I've sorted one or two things out, if that's alright by you?'

'That's super, my love,' I say and why shouldn't I? Things are improving at work; why shouldn't they improve in my private life?

After that, we spend the rest of the evening talking about the happier times we have shared in the past. When the time comes for us to leave I ask if she would like me to drop her somewhere, knowing she had arrived by taxi.'

'I was hoping you might invite me back for coffee and who knows where that could lead?' she says provocatively, spurred on by the effects of the wine.

It requires no further discussion and we are soon heading home where our lovemaking is once more filled with joy and passion. It is well into the early hours of the morning by the time we melt into satisfied sleep.

In my dreams I am making love to my wife, but this time she looks remarkably like Juanita.

'Why are you here?' I ask her.

'I am just doing my job, Robert.'

Next morning I drive Val to the railway station. I wait with her on the platform until the train to Grantham pulls in and we kiss before she climbs aboard. I stay on the platform, waving. The train pulls out of the station and I am left alone looking down the track.

I am about to turn and walk back to my car when my attention is drawn to the high-speed train pulling in on the opposite platform. The station announcer declares it is the ten-thirty from London. I watch absentmindedly as people disembark the carriages. For a moment, I catch a glimpse of one of the passengers; for one brief instant I believe I see Juanita.

I scrutinise the platform to see if I can see her again, but whoever she was is gone and I make my way back to the car. On my way home, I decide I will collect my clubs and go for a game of golf; it will be the first time I've been to the course since Colin Dalrymple became a dentist's dream-patient.

I dash into the house, change, grab my golf bag from the garage, and am back in the BMW within ten minutes and heading for my club. I decide to take a short cut I know through town.

As I head down a busy duel-carriageway approaching a large pedestrian footbridge I happen to look up and, for one second, I imagine I can see Juanita walking across it. I cruise beneath the bridge and try to look through my rear view mirror to see if I can see her again but the vision has evaporated.

At the club, I decide to forgo the round of golf, even though Gareth Handley, an old mate and a retired solicitor has thrown down a challenge. I'm too preoccupied with the visions of Juanita that have plagued me since Val left. Is it my guilty subconscious clicking in, now that I am reconciled with my wife? On the other hand, is it my inner desires pleading for Juanita to come and satiate my carnal lust?

I'm sitting in the lounge of the club enjoying a half-pint of beer and contemplating these visions when I hear a familiar and unwelcome voice.

'So, you're a drinker then?' says Lowbridge, walking through the lounge and looking as if she's just finished a round.

'Why? Is it forbidden?'

'Not forbidden,' she says, in her usual smug conceited manner, 'just frowned upon in certain circles.'

I would be annoyed if it was my best friend who had walked over and interrupted my meditations. The fact that it was Lowbridge who was ruining my Sunday afternoon is starting to make my blood boil.

'Listen, Ms Lowbridge, I'd rather not talk to you on my day off if you don't mind. I was sitting here quite happily, minding my own business, when low and behold you decide to stick your unwanted nose in my direction. I might have to put up with you being a member of this club, but I do not have to put up with listening to your incessant babbling so, if you don't mind, kindly leave me alone.'

I see a trace of anger flash in her eyes and I know she'd love to do battle with me there and then, but she knows I am right, she has no power over me here. She shrugs her shoulders and walks off, but not before…

'You're in for a heck of a shock very soon, Pike,' she states.

'Oh, you think?' I answer, emulating the playground talk of the kids at school.

'Oh, absolutely,' comes the smug reply, and she walks away.

My earlier good mood has abandoned me; Sunday is turning out to be an unpleasant day. I said goodbye to my wife after a night of ecstasy then I began seeing apparitions of the woman who has become the focus of my fantasies. Being rudely interrupted from my meditations by my despised nemesis is more than I can tolerate. I decide to go home.

As I drive home in my BMW it begins to rain and by the time I pull onto the drive it is torrential. I jump out of the car and make a dash for the front door. I have the key in the lock and am about to open it when I hear my name being called.

'Mr Pike, I wondered how long I'd need to wait.'

I turn to see a small familiar figure emerging from the bushes at the front of the house; it is Daniel Webster.

'Daniel, what the hell are you doing here?'

'I've got some news you might like to hear.'

I look round quickly to check no one is watching.

'Don't worry, nobody knows I'm here. I'm very good at what I do.'

'Well then, you'd better come in out of the rain,' I say and usher him into the porch.

Once inside I go upstairs and get two towels. Moments later I'm back and throw one to the youngster. In the lounge I tell him to sit down.

'What's so important that it can't wait until tomorrow?' I ask him as I vigorously dry my hair with the towel.

'I just came to tell you that you're going to be set up.'

'Set up? What do you mean by "set up"?' I ask. 'Set up by whom?'

'That Lowbridge woman,' he replies.

I stop drying my hair; now I'm interested.

'What do you know?'

'You're going to be accused of assaulting a school kid.'

'What?' That's ridiculous.'

His words are so preposterous I almost burst out laughing.

'How on earth have you come by this information?' I ask him, a smile on my face.

'Because I'm the kid.'

I stop laughing. The situation has suddenly become all too real. I'm on my own with a young boy from my school in my house on Sunday afternoon.

'I don't understand what you mean, Daniel. I think you need to explain.'

'It's very simple,' he calmly replies. 'She found out I'd been taking money off you in exchange for information.'

'How the hell did she find out?'

'I told her.'

'You did what?'

'I told her because I reckoned she might pay more than you did; she said she'd give me a hundred if I'd agree to her plan and claim I'd been assaulted by you.'

I stood before him, dumbfounded. This conspiracy could cause me to lose much more than my job and, if successful, would probably end up with a hefty prison sentence. There would be no defence I could put up to counter this. Lowbridge had said I had a shock coming and she was right.

'You'd better get out of here,' I say to the boy. 'Get out now.'

'Now don't go getting yourself all wound up, sir. If I was going to play along with her plan I wouldn't have come here to warn you.'

'What's that supposed to mean?' I ask him.

'She might have paid me more, but you said you'd help my mom and that means far more to me. I thought you could make the whole thing backfire on her when she tries to make the allegations stick on you.'

He is a sharp operator indeed. First he betrays my confidence, and then he betrays hers.

'Explain please, Daniel.'

'First of all, she doesn't know I'm here. She wants me to come to your office with a message on Monday morning. The message sent will be intended to upset you and make you very angry. You're supposed to get so angry that I can claim you struck me several times. The plan is that I run out of your office screaming, probably I'll tear my shirt and bang my head up against the wall for effect. Then I run through the corridors crying, like this,' he says, then burst out in to floods of very believable tears, 'until I'm found by a member of staff.'

'And how could we make this backfire?'

'Simple,' he replies, 'I just deny it was you and claim it was her.'

'But you'll be in my office,' I state, seeing a loophole in his deceit.

'Only after I've been to Lowbridge's first,' he shrugs. 'If I'm careful, no one will know whose office I came out of when I'm found running around the corridors, and if people do see me leaving your office then I'll tell them I came to you for help, but I was so frightened I ran away crying.'

'You would do all this?' I ask him.

'Yeah, of course I would,' he replies. 'I like you, sir, but I don't like that big evil looking bitch. You helped me with my mom, but that Lowbridge woman is only interested in hurting you.'

'Do you think you could carry it off?'

'Of course I could, sir,' he replies confidently, 'but it will cost you two hundred and fifty, up front.'

So here we have it, the sting in the tail, the double crosser's double crossing scheme is to squeeze as much money out of the pair of us as he can and he won't stop here. He'll probably go back to her and demand more money; we're both vulnerable and he has us both where he wants us. It's my own fault of course; I should never have thought I could trust him. Now I will need to be on my toes if I'm to out think such a crafty operator.

'I'll give you the money when you come to my office tomorrow,' I answer. 'That way I can be certain you will keep to your word.'

'Don't worry, sir; I won't let you down.'

I see him to the door and watch as he makes his way down the drive and away from the house.

'Till tomorrow then, young Webster.'

CHAPTER 12

AN UNWHOLESOME ALLIANCE AND THE VISION RETURNS

"I once said cynically of a politician, He'll double-cross that bridge when he comes to it."
Oscar Levant

I'm on edge. I'm so on edge that I didn't even go to the staff briefing this morning.

I'm sitting in my office waiting for Daniel to arrive. I am clear in my mind as to what I have to do. I spent a sleepless night planning for today. I have a particular dislike for Mondays; a dislike I share in common with many who work for their living, but today could prove to be the most disagreeable Monday of my career. My monumental stupidity in trusting Webster in the first place could be paid for in my own blood if he decides to fly his colours in my enemy's camp.

Right now she is probably sitting in her office thinking the same thing. In fairness though, she was drawn into this by necessity; once Webster had disclosed our little secret she had to move. She could have gone for me then and there, but if we both denied everything she knew there would be those who would speculate that she was trying to tarnish my name in order to meet her own ends. No, it has to be played out this way because things have already gone too far.

A knock at my door indicates the game is about to start.

'Come in!' I shout and I am not surprised to see Daniel open the door and enter.

'Hello, sir,' he says with a broad smile on his face. 'I've brought you a message from Miss Lowbridge.'

He hands me the paper. I take it and read what is written:

I need to discuss staffing cuts for next year. We need to save a considerable amount of money to balance the budget. You will come to a meeting promptly at 9am tomorrow morning.

K L

So this is the message meant to send me into a mad uncontrollable frenzy. Her intention is obvious; she thinks she can provoke me into a rage through subtly suggesting she might be thinking of getting rid of me or maybe expecting me to be angered by the tone of the message. Either way, if you couple my supposed rage with a distraught child, who has a bruised head and torn clothes, it is easy to see how Lowbridge would have the sort of solid evidence on which to base a case for my dismissal.

'Have you got the money?' he asks eagerly. 'Only the price has gone up to three hundred.'

I have been developing my skills as a devious bastard since long before this little tyke was even a small blip on the radar. Fortunately, therefore, I had foreseen this inevitable inflation and made certain I had enough cash at my disposal.

From my desk draw I take out a wad of notes. I also take out an old envelope. I count out the money, place it into the envelope and hand it to him.

'Thank you, sir,' he says, as he stuffs the packet into his back pocket. 'I'd better get ready for the next part.'

Casually he tears at his sweater and then, as he's walking to the door, he whacks his head sharply against the wall.

'I'll wait till the coast is clear then go. I shan't start crying until I'm closer to her office,' he states as he opens the door slightly and looks to check that no one is on the corridor. When satisfied that the coast is clear he's off and another scene on this surreal Monday ends.

I wait a short time then I, too, leave the sanctity of my room and head off towards Ms Lowbridge's office.

It takes several minutes to walk the length of the school to the area near the main entrance which is occupied by the administration staff and the Headteacher. By the time I arrive a large group of staff has already gathered around the whimpering and wailing Master Daniel Webster.

He is being consoled by Shirley Makepeace and Bev Munroe, Daniel's Head of Year. The other onlookers are mainly support assistants and office staff, whose names I've either forgotten or not even bothered to get to know in the first place. Best of all however, standing at the open door of her office, is the ashen faced Katherine Lowbridge.

'She attacked me,' screams Daniel. I have to admit, he is very good at this. 'She got angry and said she was going to kill me. She hit me lots, but I escaped and ran to Sir's office to tell him.'

My timing is perfect. I arrive just as his Oscar winning performance has reached the point where I am able to deliver the Coup De Gras. He sees me.

'Sir, tell them what happened!'

Lowbridge is standing by her door shaking her head and saying things to the staff. I can see she is incredibly agitated, but the boy's performance is so good that no one pays her any attention.

I have her now! All I have to do is corroborate his story and she would be finished. No Governing body or Local Authority in the country would protect her from the inevitable consequences.

She's staring at me; she knows I have her. She knows I can destroy her and she's helpless. I savour the moment. Should I make her suffer more? No, the time has come to end it.

'Ah Mrs Makepeace, you've got him,' I say, my words well rehearsed.

Shirley, a person of great professional integrity, looks at me with bewildered eyes; she can't quite believe the enormity of the events taking place.

'He says he's been assaulted,' she tells me, then casts an accusing glance in the direction of Lowbridge. 'He says that he came to you and you can back up his claim. He said he was so upset he even ran from your office. Mr Pike is it true?'

'Yes, he came to my office and yes, he ran away from it, but I wasn't there when he arrived; I'd just nipped to the toilet and left my office door unlocked. He was certainly in there alright and now an envelope with three hundred pounds of school funds is missing from my desk. Luckily, I saw him stuffing it into his back pocket as he ran away, just as I was on my way back from the toilet. Look and see, it must still be there.'

Shirley, a highly experienced practitioner in dealing with problem children, deftly reaches down and snatches the envelope from Daniel's back pocket.

'It's still in the school-fund envelope,' says Shirley as she reads the faded printing.

Instantly young Webster realises the double crosser has been double crossed and desperately tries to ad lib. It is, of course, the worst plan of action he could adopt.

'He gave it me and told me to grass her up,' he screams, pointing from me to Lowbridge.

I shake my head and display a face of sympathy and understanding.

'Daniel, Daniel, don't make it worse for yourself,' I say in a pleading voice, knowing that this time it will be me receiving the acting honours.

Daniel becomes frantic and the name calling and swearing starts. He is soon consumed by his own irrationality and he digs a deeper and deeper hole. I maneuver him into an interview room and we call the staff at his care home to come and escort from the premises.

It's over. All that's left to do is the mopping up. Tomorrow the Headteacher, with my recommendation, will permanently exclude the boy; there probably won't even be an appeal. Sometime later the Governors will ratify the exclusion. The police have also been informed and the incident may well be added to his file of misdemeanours. Daniel played a dangerous game and he failed.

As for my own actions, how can I explain what I did? Why, when I had 'Her' throat under my boot, did I not crush it there and then when for days, weeks and months I have been plagued by her, threatened by her and bullied by her?

I did what I did for one reason and one reason only. On Sunday afternoon when Daniel Webster arrived at my house I realised it was he who was my greatest threat and that Lowbridge would have to wait. She obviously didn't see the danger when she decided to play by the rules I had adopted; once more her arrogance is clearly demonstrated. What I couldn't do is allow a little snot like Daniel have control over us, no matter how much I loathe and detest her. When I do defeat her I want it to be done my way, with my strategy and by my own hand.

As for Daniel? Well, he could have been a useful ally but greed took control. He'll say we were involved and that we gave him money, but at the end of the day who would people prefer to believe, a delinquent kid with a record as long as your arm or two highly respected members of society? It's over now and I doubt Lowbridge will never mention the matter to me again and I will certainly not raise the issue with her.

I'm at home again, happy and contented once more. Scary Sunday gave way to Manic Monday, but I survived and that is, beyond any shadow of a doubt, the most important thing.

I lie here mulling over the day's events. One thing still puzzles me: as I was pulling out of the car park and onto the main road I was sure I saw Juanita getting in to Toby Marriott's MG.   What is happening to me? Why am I haunted by these visions of her? Maybe I've been working too hard suffering from stress; it would be understandable. Perhaps I should consult a shrink.

I dream I am cuddled up in bed with a woman. She whispers words of devotion and kisses me tenderly. I'm in love with her and I know it, but I don't understand how this can be. She has the lithe supple golden skinned body of Juanita and the grace, charm, style and wit of my lovely wife Valerie, but why, oh why, does she look like Jeremy Paxman?'

CHAPTER 13

THE BANDIDO AND MY CHIQUITA

"Anyone who says that gratuitous sex is no substitute for gratuitous violence obviously hasn't had enough gratuitous sex."
Geoff Spear

It's Tuesday again and that means staff briefing. I can hardly contain my excitement. I stand next to the Headteacher and wait with baited breath to marvel at the array of wonderfully important appointments she may be sharing with us today. Will it be an in-depth discussion with the School Meals Service about the tricky decision as to whether to provide apple or orange juice at break time or will it be the monumentally important monthly meeting with the local primary Headteachers? Having attended many of these meetings I know they will spend their valuable time deciding which of them will provide the custard creams at the next vitally important meeting. Who cares? I'm in such an amazingly vibrant mood I may even pay attention to what she has to say today.

While I wait for the fun to begin I scan the staffroom. It's always the same faces sitting in the same places. There is Shirley Makepeace, stationed near the door just in case one of her little charges have a crisis; Derek Forrest is in his usual corner, demonstrating another lame-brained theory on paper to another unwitting victim; Bev Monroe is looking as radiant as ever (how does she get boobs that big under her sweater?); next to her, and transfixed by her Grand Canyon proportioned cleavage, sits the bronzed form of Gino Colletti, a one time tight-rope artist and circus acrobat turned PE teacher. It occurs to me that some staff must have been sitting in the same chair for twenty-five years or more! I continue to scan the room. A few seats away from Gino I notice Tanya Raymond sitting quietly studying a map of the school, obviously still trying to allocate forty life-sized decorated concrete cows whilst just to her right Toby Marriott is laughing and joking with Juanita Cortez.

... Juanita Cortez! I knew it! I've been working under far too much pressure; I've finally flipped and am hallucinating. In my state of madness I see my Andalucian beauty sitting in my staffroom chatting to the King of the Lounge Lizards.

The apparition sees me and immediately stops laughing and talking to Marriott. She looks at me, bewildered, and I see that she is saying something; is it my name? Is she saying "Robert"?

I don't hear a word of the Headteacher's morning oration and, whilst there is nothing unusual in this, the source of my ignorance is not usually the unexpected presence of my Iberian lover.

Someone is speaking to me, but my mind is in so much of a spin I hear only gobbledygook. The apparition looks embarrassed and she shuffles awkwardly in her chair. I'm aware that everyone in the staffroom is staring in my direction; even Derek Forrest has stopped gabbling and is looking straight at me. Someone speaks to me again. It is Lowbridge; the sharpness of her words brings me back to the meeting.

'Is there anything you want to say, Mister Pike?'

It's my turn to speak, my turn to add to briefing, but I am confused and cannot think straight. My mind is in a spin and my pulse is racing. I know in this state I should keep quiet and say nothing, but my mouth is too quick for me and too eager to be filled by my foot.

'Juanita, I love you,' I blurt out.

The first time in living memory a staff briefing ended in laughter was when Mr Shilling, a previous Headteacher, informed the staff that a minibus full of OFSTED inspectors on its way to the school to carry out a week long interrogation had been involved in a head-on collision with a tanker full of liquid manure. Muted sniggering gave way to a thunderous display of amusement and cheering by the time the Head announced there had been no survivors. Today was to be the second.

I turn to see Lowbridge looking at me down her long lupine snout with utter disgust as the rest of the staff whoop and whistle; a few even shout out "We love you too, Bob" which only makes Her Royal Ugliness even more angry.

'Mr Pike, I will see you in my office at 9 o'clock.'

I acknowledge her demand without debate; my mind is still in a whirl. I am perplexed as to what might be happening to me.

By the time I start to recover my sanity, the bell for the start of the day has clanged and the staffroom is emptying. The vision of Juanita leaves and I am compelled to follow. Like a love-struck adolescent romantic I follow her until she arrives at the modern languages area. She's talking to Andrea Freeman, the Head of the department, as I walk up to her and catch her by the elbow to steer her away from the bemused member of staff.

I guide her round the corner, out of the main flow of children making their way to registration.

'It's you,' I say, somewhat stating the bloody obvious. 'It really is you.'

'Yes, it is me,' she replies and then tries to push past me, but I block her way.

'What the hell are you doing here?' I demand.

She drops her eyes to the floor and looks embarrassed and awkward.

'I'm the new Spanish exchange teacher,' she says.

'But how can you be?' I reply, about to make a total ass of myself. 'You're a bullfighter's assistant.'

'No I am not, Robert,' she says, shame etched on her face.

'You lied to me?' I reply, from my lofty perch in Castle Bombastic on moral high-ground. I feel offended and hurt at being treated in such a way.

'A stuntman?' she answers and I tumble from my battlements of self-righteousness and slide down the slope of arrogance.

We stare at each other for a few seconds then the pair of us burst out laughing, highly amused at the ridiculous situation to which our creative minds have brought us.

'I thought I was seeing things,' I eventually manage to say.

'So did I,' she replies. 'I say to myself, I know him! He and I we... you know... together.'

Again we laugh, but I am conscious we are still on public view.

'Look, what are you doing tonight? Maybe we can go for dinner… together.'

Her face registers sympathy and disappointment at the same time, but probably not in the same quantities reflected in mine when I hear her reply.

'I would love to, Robert, but I've already said I would go out with Toby, he is such a nice boy. He has been kind enough to give up his bedroom for me during my stay.'

I'm on my way to the meeting with Lowbridge. The words Juanita spoke to me a few moments ago have left me furious; Juanita is soon to be another victim of that conniving shit, Marriott.

I storm down each corridor snapping and snarling at anyone and everything that moves. By design I make sure that my path to her room takes me past Marriott's teaching area. He's in the process of starting his lesson with a year 8 class when I barge in.

'I want to see you in my office at break time today, Mr Marriott,' I almost shout. 'Is that understood?'

'I'm on duty at break,' he answers.

'Forget your duty and be in my office, clear?'

He nods and I can see in his face he's more than a little nervous. Good, let the swine sweat, let him suffer until ten-thirty and then let him suffer some more. I slam the door as I leave his room and then scream at two pupils sauntering along the corridor. They can see from my demeanour that any surly behaviour on their part might not be the best course of action and they scamper away to the safety of their classroom.

I'm now five minutes late for my meeting with Lowbridge, but I do not care one iota. I don't even bother to knock on her door.

'You wanted to see me?' I say as I enter; she's not alone.

Sitting opposite her is Tanya Raymond; they are both studying a plan of the school laid out before them on the glass-topped desk.

'I'm just speaking to Tanya about the location of our cows,' says the great Amazonian, without bothering to look in my direction.

'You asked to see me now,' I snap. 'I haven't got the time to waste waiting for you to finish talking about concrete bloody cattle.'

Now she looks at me. Now I have her attention. Methodically she folds the plan up and hands it back to the uneasy head of art.

'We'll talk later, Tanya. I think some of your ideas are very exciting,' she says, in that sickly, syrupy condescending way of hers.

Tanya makes a hasty exit, realising she may be about to get caught between two warring titans. The sigh of relief she gives is audible to the pair of us as she closes the office door.

'Don't you ever come into my office like that again... ,' she begins.

'Don't start lecturing me,' I snap. 'You wanted to see me now, so don't act all offended when I arrive on time.'

'You are late,' she replies. 'Poor punctuality is not professional.'

'Oh, for-crying-out-loud! Do you want to speak to me or not? If you do then tell what it's about and stop all this crap!'

I've fired both barrels, but she's far from bereft of ammunition and is soon blasting me with unerring accuracy.

'Your behaviour in briefing this morning was outrageous. First of all you ignore me and then you start shouting out words of love to a new member of staff!' she counters. 'Do I need to start questioning your state of mind?'

I've heard enough. This is not the best day she could have chosen to threaten me.

'Do what you need to and stop making your bloody threats. Just remember, I can dish the dirt as well as you can so if it's a war you want then bring it on. I'm sick of your constant threats and bullying.'

For the second time today a door frame and its hinges suffer as a result of my temper. I stomp through the corridors back to my office, snarling at every pupil and glaring at every member of staff. Only when I pass the modern languages rooms and see Juanita in one of them teaching a class of year 7 pupils does my mood heal and a sense of well-being permeate my body. As I move past the room so passes the feeling of well-being and I am once more the evil Hyde as opposed to the calm and sensitive Jekyll.

Back in my office I stomp and fume. I need to release my anger, but there is still five minutes to survive until my ten-thirty appointment. I don't usually suffer such bouts of rage, but the thought of my little Juanita in the clutches of such a predatory beast as Toby Marriott sends my blood way past boiling point. Still, I understand that I will need to appear relaxed and at ease when he arrives. It's important for him to incriminate himself before I decide where to take the situation.

The five minutes take an age to pass, but eventually there is a knock on my door.

'Come in,' I say, sounding as composed as I possibly can.

'You wanted to see me, Bob?' he says as he pops his head round the edge of the door.

'Yes, come in Toby and take a chair. Sorry I was a bit terse this morning. I'd just had a run in with some of the smokers behind the rubbish bins; you know how it is,' I reply; the act of making an apology tearing my insides to shreds.

He sits and a look of relief spreads over his features.

'That's okay, Bob,' he says. 'For one moment I thought you were really bloody angry with me.'

'No, no Toby, not at all.'

An awkward pause follows in which we just stare at each other. He's waiting for me to speak, but what he doesn't realise is that the very sight of him is making me want to strangle the breath out of him.

'I hear you've got the new Spanish exchange teacher staying with you.' I say, trying my hardest to sound nonchalant.

'Juanita Cortez, yes,' he answers. 'That was bloody funny what you said this morning Bob, straight out of the blue like that. She was so embarrassed. I told her you probably had the hots for her. Mind you, I wouldn't blame you; what a gorgeous little body. I think I've fallen on my feet with this one. I'm taking her out tonight and afterwards I thought...'

As he has been talking I've walked round my desk and before he can complete the sentence I grab him by his lapels and haul him to his feet.

'For Christ's sake, Bob! What's got into you?'

'You little shit, you so much as lay a hand on her and I kill you. Do you hear me?'

I'm not usually prone to acts of violence, but I know how to get physical when I need to. For many years I played rugby at a relatively high level. Some well connected people in the game said I was destined for great things, but a serious knee injury at the age of twenty-two curtailed any ambitions I had and I had to satisfy myself with remaining a good second-eleven club player. A little voice inside my head is telling me that now is as good a time as any to get physical and vent my rage.

Every ounce of his breath leaves his body with a satisfying wail and this time I allow his body to seek the comfort of the floor, but slightly less gently than he would've liked.

'I'm mad alright and you'll soon find out just how mad if you don't do as you've been told. Mention anything about this to anyone and I'll have your career. I'll tell people I found it impossible to keep my hands off you when I discovered what you'd been up to with certain members of our school fraternity, understand?'

He looks up at me through eyes filled with pain and fear.

'You bastard,' he mumbles.

'Acknowledged,' I say as I grab a decent handful of his blonde locks and twist with a good deal of satisfied pleasure. 'You do as you're told and there will be no problem, but if you fuck about with me I'll do more than punch you in the nuts; I'll see that they're removed completely.'

The bell indicating the end of break sounds.

'Ah, saved by the bell,' I say as I haul him to his feet. 'Take my advice Toby and go to see your sick mother. Don't worry about us here, we'll cope without you and I'll see you sometime next week.'

Toby left my office. I feel better now, much better. Perhaps every now and then I should let go of my aggression. Having given up rugby I need to find another way to express my hidden rage; I can't very well just take it out on poor Toby every time I feel like venting my boiler.

My earlier ill temper has now been replaced by sheer contentment. Once Toby informed Juanita that dinner was cancelled due to his need to visit his mother and told her that she would not be able to lodge with him during her stay she, understandably, needed to turn to someone for help. That person, of course, was me; I made it so by making sure I was on hand at the right time. Not that she complained, in fact she looked positively delighted with the outcome.

Just right now she's sitting next to me in the BMW as I drive the familiar route home. In the boot is the case of her belongings Toby Marriott kindly fetched from his flat before scooting off to be at the bedside of his ailing mother.

Her perfume has the same intoxicating effect as when I first met her and this further improves my mood as we chat during our journey; my eyes occasionally stray from watching the road to her perfectly formed golden legs and her exquisite breasts. She has a bewitching effect on me like no other women I have ever known. I cannot keep my eyes off her and, as I turn into my drive, I imagine the night of ecstasy to come. All too late I see the bright new Mini. I slam my foot on the brake, but there is nothing I can do to avoid the inevitable collision. Juanita looks horrified as, without thinking, I put the motor into reverse, pull away from the collision and make a hasty getaway down the street; a good proportion of the Mini still attached to the front of my car. In my efforts to wrest my little Chiquita from the clutches of such a rampant sexual bandit I'd forgotten all about Val coming home.

'Oh bollocks!'

CHAPTER 14

OF TEXT MESSAGES, SOOTHSAYERS
AND SEA NYMPHS

*"The Grand essentials of happiness are: something to do,
something to love, and something to hope for."*
Allan K. Chalmers

The text message on my mobile phone from Val reads:

I h8 u. I nvr wnt 2 c u agn

It's taken me several minutes to interpret what on earth she is saying. I suppose it is only to be expected as I have now written-off another brand new car of hers.

I'm sitting in a restaurant waiting for our coffees to arrive. Juanita has just skipped off to the ladies to powder her nose. I must say, I'm surprised it has taken this long for Val to contact me. She will be furious. What can I say? My jealousy over one woman has probably cost me the chance of rescuing my relationship with another. What should I do next?

The sight of Juanita walking back to me provides me with my answer. She moves with such a playful elegance I'm bewitched every time I am in her company. Neither the incident on the driveway or my desperation to escape the scene has managed to dampen the evening's proceedings. She seems very comfortable in my company and eager to remain so.

Our coffee arrives soon after she sits down.

'So tell me, Robert, where am I going to sleep tonight if your ex-wife has decided to move back into your house?'

I'd told Juanita that Val and I were separated and had no idea she would be at the house. The story seemed to satisfy her, but her question requires a resolution, and not just for Juanita.

'I thought we'd check in to a hotel.'

She is happy with this and after we finish our coffee I settle the bill and we make our way back to the car. With one headlight and indicator light completely trashed it would be foolhardy to drive in the dark, especially as I have over half a bottle of red in my system. I decide to call a taxi.

It's only when we are half way across town on the way to the hotel that we realise her case and the emergency change of clothes I keep to hand have been left in the BMW. We contemplate asking the taxi to turn round but decide it is not the end of the world and I can return to the car first thing in the morning. Besides, the butterflies of expectation and excitement are beginning to flap their wings furiously in my gut and I am impatient to experience the thrill of passionate lovemaking.

At the reception desk we check in and I order a bottle of red to be sent up to the room. As we head up to the third floor in the lift I find it hard to contain myself. I want to hold her and squeeze her and kiss her, but I manage to refrain. Once inside the room I can contain myself no longer. Our embrace seems to last forever. She finally breaks away and begins to unbutton my shirt.

'Time for my big bull to take a shower,' she says as she pulls off my jacket and seductively peels my shirt over my shoulders. 'I will undress you then you take a shower. I come and join you; is that okay?'

Is that okay? Is she joking? Just the thought is enough to make me burst with excitement. Hurriedly I help her remove my clothes and obediently go in to the bathroom. I turn on the shower and step in; my mood is so good I begin to sing.

'You're just too good to be true...'

I complete three verses and four choruses before it occurs to me that Juanita is taking more time than expected to join me in the shower.

I step out of the cubicle, grab a towel and go in to the room. The red wine has been delivered; it sits, with two glasses, on a silver platter on the dressing table. Juanita is in the room, but only just; she is standing in the open doorway with my clothes a crumpled heap in her arms.

'Who do you think you are, huh?' she snarls. 'You think I don't know what you did to poor Toby? You think you can change my plans without asking me?'

'But I thought...' I begin to babble.

'Bah, you men, you think with this,' she says pointing to my groin, 'and not with the head.'

'Juanita, what's wrong with you?'

'There is nothing wrong with me, hombre,' she snaps, 'but there is plenty wrong with you. You treat Toby badly and you treat your wife badly and then you expect me to come and jump into your bed. Well you are an ass-hole and I'm gonna teach you a lesson.'

I suddenly realise what she intends to do and make a dash for her, but in doing so I lose my grip on the towel and it slips to the floor. She has seen me make my move and disappears into the corridor. She runs towards the lifts and stairs. I chase her, but she is too quick for me and she skips through the fire door and into to stairwell.

I'm totally naked; I can't follow her. I turn around to go back to the room to get the towel and that's when I hear the door click shut.

'You Spanish bitch!'

I'm helpless; naked, locked out and at a loss for any ideas as what to do. I'm on the verge of panic when I hear the lift at the end of the corridor stop on this floor. The doors slide open. I have nowhere to run, nowhere to hide; I'm about to face yet another massive humiliation.

I can hear people chatting in the lift; I even see the first foot appear around the corner. I am sweating but motionless with fear.

'Quickly, come in here!'

The door opposite has opened. There is no alternative but to comply and I dive through the door and in to the darkened room beyond; the door shuts behind me and I lie on the floor, the only damage I have sustained are two carpet burns to my knees.

'You're late,' a voice says in the dark.'

My eyes have not yet adjusted to the blackness of the room, but I begin to make out the form of a person sitting in front of the closed curtains next to the bed.

'Thanks,' I say as I get to my feet and cup my hands around my genitalia. 'I locked myself out of my room, so

I'd be really grateful if you would call reception and have someone send up a spare key.'

'You were sent here for a purpose.'

The voice seems to be that of an old woman with a central European accent. I can hear Lowbridge in my head telling me that it is not very professional to be caught breaking in to an old Hungarian Lady's hotel bedroom at one o'clock in the morning. This is turning into a very bad night indeed.

'I can assure you that no one sent me. I just happened to be locked out of my room, without my clothes,' even as I say it my heart sinks. How long before this old lady comprehends her mistake and starts screaming?

'You are Robert Pike and you have been sent here to listen to my words.'

Now I'm more than spooked. How does she know my name and how did she know I'd be here tonight?
'I'm sorry, but have we met before?'

I try to make out more detail in the darkness, but although my eyes have grown accustomed to the low level of light, the room is so well blacked-out that all I can see is the still dim outline of the seated figure.

'You will soon have a choice to make; one that will mean joy for some and heartbreak for others. One who is dead will give you much and one that lives will seek to take much from you. A loved one will return and you shall know boundless pleasure, free from the shackles that have kept your lust at bay.'

I'm compelled to listen even though I appear to be in the bedroom of some nutter who is probably about to charge at me wielding a carving knife.

'For many years you will know fame and fortune but a small child will be your undoing. You will fall from grace.'

She's obviously mad, but I can't help myself from asking a question.

'Tell me, are these the shadows of what will come or are they shadows of what may come and can I change my future?' I sound like Scrooge speaking to one of his ghosts. 'Look, Mrs Whoeveryouare, I'm really grateful for you helping me out, but I need to call reception and get a key for my room.'

I move close to the bed where I imagine the phone to be and fumble around in the dark. Eventually my hand touches the familiar shape of a handset. Eagerly I pick up the receiver and feel the buttons to find the 0 key. Satisfied I have found it I press it; nothing happens, the phone is dead.

I turn back to face the shape by the window, but it has gone. Now I begin to panic; she's moving towards me with the knife raised and I can't see her. Fear takes over and I try to run towards the door, but as I do I collide with a chair and tumble to the ground. My head connects with something hard and I lose consciousness.

I'm drifting on a sea of deepest blue in a boat of shimmering gold. In the sky soft clouds of glittering silver gently move towards the land on the horizon. In the sea I hear splashing and look over the edge of my small craft to see a beautiful woman swimming playfully just beneath the waves. When she sees me she heads upwards, breaks through the surface of the water and leaps onto my boat; she is totally naked and without doubt the most beautiful woman I have ever seen. Her skin is the colour of the purest cream and her long golden hair sparkles with the reflection of the sun. Her eyes are the colour of deepest jade and her lips red and full.

'I'm waiting for you, my love,' she says. 'Don't be long, I need you soon. I want you so much my heart is on fire for you.'

Without saying another word the stunning sea nymph jumps back in to the water and circles my little boat before diving beneath the surface. I wave to her and wish her to return, but she is gone and I am alone once more.

Suddenly my boat is pitched violently back and forth as from below the waves erupts the long green scaly neck of a sea serpent. The neck is topped with a hideous head that is the spitting, slavering, drooling image of Katherine Lowbridge.

Relentlessly the great slimy beast moves towards me; its wet lips smacking as it anticipates a main course of Pike a la mode. I desperately try to paddle away from the beast, but I am too slow and its horrendous jaws open and descend, engulfing my whole body.

Slowly I am sucked down the gullet of the monster and towards its putrid great belly. I struggle and kick and punch, but the things throat is beginning to tighten about my body; I start screaming.

I am still screaming when I wake up. It takes me a while to unwrap myself from the bedclothes, but when I do I realise I'm back in my own room in the hotel. The bottle of red still sits on the silver tray, but it is empty with only a small residue of the liquid it contained left in each of the wine glasses. My wallet is where Juanita left it as are my car keys, but more remarkably the bag of spare clothes I keep in the boot of the BMW is lying on the dressing table next to the wine bottle and glasses.

I climb out of bed, my head hurts like hell, and stumble into the bathroom where I discover the source of the pain. In the bathroom mirror I see a large jagged gash running down the side of my forehead. There is a round swelling beneath and congealed blood along the length of broken skin.

'What happened last night?' I ask myself.

Did Juanita return and help me to bed, fetch my clothes and drink the wine? A nice thought, but I severely doubt it. What about the mysterious old woman in the other room? I remember hitting my head when I fell, but what happened after? Did she get me back in this room, then fetch my clothes and drink the wine? Again, it seems highly unlikely besides, two wine glasses were used last night. Perhaps the best thing would be to be direct and knock on the door of the room opposite and see if anyone answers.

With my mind made up I shower, this time taking my clothes with me, bathe the gash on my head and clean away the congealed blood as best as possible. Next I dress and comb my hair.

When at last I feel almost presentable I grab my wallet and keys and leave the room. The door behind which I found sanctuary last night is directly opposite. Without hesitating I step across the corridor and knock twice on the door.

After a few seconds I hear the latch pulled and the door swings open. A young woman stands there. She is wearing a smart grey business suit.

'Can I help you?' she asks with a strong Swedish accent.

The unexpected sight of this tall elegant beautiful woman throws me completely and I begin to babble like an imbecile.

'Ah, yes, night last, you did me see?'

'I'm sorry,' she replies, with a kind and sympathetic voice.

I try my best to regain some composure and ask my question again.

'Were you in this room last night?'

'Yes, of course I was,' she answers, more than slightly perplexed. 'Why, is there some problem?'

'No,' I reply. 'I'm so terribly sorry to have bothered you. Please forgive me.'

She smiles kindly, if somewhat nervously and closes the door. I walk slowly down the corridor to the lift. At reception I settle the bill and ask them to call me a taxi so that I can go and fetch the BMW.

During the taxi journey I mull over the events of the last ten hours, but in doing so I am even more confused than before. When I knocked the door opposite the room we had taken in the hotel I had expected to find the old woman or no one at all. What I could not have possibly predicted was that the female who actually opened the door would turn out to be the girl from my dreams; the beautiful, golden-haired sea nymph.

CHAPTER 15

FLOWER POWER AND WAYNE **MOO**NEY

"When the power of love overcomes the love of power the world will know peace."
Jimi Hendrix

There's a concrete cow outside my office decorated to look like it is wearing a Manchester United strip with the name Mooney painted on its back above a number nine. How it got there I have no idea, it just arrived over night.

I'd noticed several other cows as I headed for the sanctuary of my office after suffering the indignity of fronting a year 7 assembly this morning. Right outside the hall is a cow decorated with painted motifs representing different cultures of the world. It is a tasteful piece of work carried out with sensitivity and style. I wish I could say the same for the pink monstrosity with a huge marijuana leaf painted on each side of its large body which has been placed directly outside the staffroom. The concrete cow in the technology area is covered with cuttings from the latest Argos catalogue whilst the sculpture at the entrance to the maths department is painted white with a simple sum of, 2+2=5, stencilled in black, running down its hind quarters.

Most of these works of art reflect the sort of outcome I would have expected from the residency we hosted with Hermann Grund. It was only when I saw the statue outside the Head's office that I was truly shocked but, at the same time, highly amused.

The cow had been painted wearing a dark business suit. On its feet the children had placed four high-heeled boots and a pair of reading glasses had been attached to the end of its nose with a glue-gun. The crowning glory however was, without doubt, the orange-bristled scrubbing brush stuck to its head. There it stood, just outside her domain; a shining testament to the impression she had made on the school community.

In many respects I feel I've got off lightly by only having the Wayne Mooney edifice stationed outside my room. Still, I shall need to have a word with someone about the actual positioning of the creature as I have to squeeze past the great horned head to get in and out.

Having just finished my impression of a limbo dancer to get into my office and attack the pile of paperwork in my in-tray the phone rings. Actually, to my utter amazement, it moos but I pick the receiver up regardless.

'Pike here.'

'Hello Mr Pike. I have a gentleman in reception who would like to see you,' says Jackie Ethelridge, one of our receptionists. 'He says he's from Slope and Glutts Solicitors and he needs to discuss a matter concerning Old Bill.'

I'm interested. For one thing it concerns Bill and secondly it's about something other than school-work.

Thirdly, I want to see some other poor devil try and negotiate the cow outside my office.

'Yes, that's fine,' I confirm. 'Send him over.'

'Thank you, Mr Pike. I'll tell him,' replies the ever courteous Jackie.

'Oh Jackie,' I say, before she replaces her receiver. 'Why did my phone moo when you rang me?'

'Oh, that's the school council,' she replies. 'They said it would be good if every phone in the school was programmed with a mooing ringtone to go with the concrete cows. We all think its fab in the office, so funny.'

'Thanks Jackie,' I say and hang up.

Several minutes go by before I hear someone puffing and panting outside my door followed by the sound of an object being dropped and several muffled curses. Eventually there is a knock on the door.

'Enter,' I say, barely able to keep the smile off my face as I see the size of my visitor.

'Ah, good day Mr Pike' says the man as he enters my room, almost filling it by doing so.

'It's a bit of a tight squeeze getting past the sculpture out there,' he puffs as he indicates the concrete cow on the other side of the door.

'Oh, really? I hadn't noticed,' I reply, still trying to maintain a straight face. 'How can I help you Mr...?'

'Mr Glutts at your service, sir,' he states and hands me his business card. 'I'm here to talk about William Arthur Trundell's last Will and Testament.'

Oh great. Old Bill's left me a collection of seed catalogues.

'As you are probably aware, Mr Trundell had accumulated an estate of some considerable wealth, mainly through his activities as Mister Rose.'

'Considerable?' I ask, knowing full well that if a solicitor describes something as considerable then it must be ... considerable.

'Considerable indeed,' says the portly man. 'Assets totalling somewhere in the region of five million pounds including cash, property and land.'

'Five million?'

I almost fall off my chair. Old Bill was a multi-millionaire and he still lived in a smelly wreck of a caravan on our site. No wonder he never bothered about asking for a pay rise.

'You have been named personally in the Will, Mr Pike.'

Suddenly I feel faint. He had no relatives so am I about to inherit a fortune? How much? How much?

'As the executor of Mr Trundell's last will and testament, I have been instructed to inform you that two million...'

'He's left me two million!' I scream, and I'm on my feet ready to dance a jig I'm so happy.

Mr Glutts, however, looks less than amused and like a true professional carries on with his duties.

'...that two million has been donated to Laburnum School with the express instruction that it must be administered by Mr Robert Pike.'

'Oh, that was very kind of him,' is all I can reply before I regain any form of composure. 'What about the rest of the five million?'

'That has been allocated to other good causes, but the largest percentage by far is given to the school.'

'No individual inheritances then?'

'Only to Mr Lavender, your school caretaker I believe?'

'Yes, that's right,' I answer, crestfallen. 'How much?'

'I'm afraid I can't disclose that information, Mr Pike, as I'm sure you are quite aware.'

We have very little more to say apart from making an appointment for me to go to the Slope and Glutts office to sign some documents that will allow the release of the money to the school. I'm too wrapped up in my own disappointment to delight in listening to Mr Glutts trying to negotiate Wayne Mooney outside.

'Five million?'

Its two o'clock and I've just received the royal summons from Lowbridge. She never thinks to get off her backside to see anyone but remains cooped up in her own lair, sending out her instructions and orders without knowing or understanding the institute she leads. She is like Sauron as she broods malevolently in her place of power, casting her evil eye this way and that until she catches sight of some innocent Hobbit she can persecute.

So here I am making my way to confront her yet again. I've made the journey so many times in the last few months and usually for the same reason; to receive another bollocking. What it will be about this time I have no idea, but I can bet two million quid it won't be anything positive.

'I've had a complaint about you,' Mr Pike,' she says once I've entered her room and taken my place in the hot seat opposite her, 'a very serious and worrying complaint.'

'Oh, yes, what have I done this time?' I reply, trying to sound as glib as possible.

'You won't find it so amusing when I tell you that I'm referring the matter to the Governors,' she states. 'The sexual harassment of a member of staff could be a dismissable offence if it can be proven.'

'And who am I supposed to have sexually harassed?'

She does not answer. Instead she just stares at me down that long nose over the wire framed spectacles perched at its end. I can see pure hatred reflected in her small piggy eyes and a hint of a sneer on her thin lipped mouth.

'You really are a despicable individual, Pike,' she eventually utters. 'I'm surprised any woman has ever wanted to get near you. You make me sick, you all do; all you womanising, lecherous, devious, self-centred bastards.'

'Is that comment on the record?' I ask as innocently as possible.

'I'm going to break you this time,' she snarls, her voice increasing in volume. 'I'm going to see you are destroyed and that you never work in anther school again. You are an abomination and you should not be tolerated. The Governors will hear the complaint and I will make my recommendations. I think it would be better if you take some gardening leave while they make their decision and I'm certain that will be to dismiss you. You will have no one to blame but yourself.'

'That would be a real shame,' I reply; my Dogs of War primed and ready to let slip, 'considering it would cost the school two million pounds.'

'What on earth are you talking about?'

'Only that I have, today, been named as the sole administrator for a two million pound donation to the School. So if I'm not here, no one will benefit from the money and just think, I could have wiped out our large budget deficit, saved jobs and had the school extended and improved, but you go ahead and try to get me removed, I'm certain the Governor's will be grateful.'

I go on to tell her the full detail of the Trundell donation, even showing her some of the paper work Mr Glutts left with me concerning the Will.

By the end of our meeting she has, unsurprisingly, changed her tune and decided to deal with the matter of the complaint from a member of staff "behind closed doors;" a Headteacher's way of saying that nothing further will happen. She has even given me the nature of the complaint and its source. It was, as I suspected, Juanita.

As I walk away from the Beast's office I realise once more I have been fortunate in my war with her. How often I can keep surviving her onslaught remains to be seen, but it may be that one day soon I will need to take the offensive and attack her.

'It's shocking,' says Tom Lavender as we stand looking at the caravan once occupied by Old Bill Trundell.

It has changed considerably since I last saw it, but then again that was before Hermann Grund, the Anglo/Austrian artist decided to take a hand. Even the thought of the blonde Goliath makes my backside smart, even after all these weeks.

'We can't leave this here; it's a bloody eyesore, Bob.'

What he says is true, as the once sombre green caravan has now been decorated with every colour of the rainbow. Hundreds of bright hand-painted flower heads now adorn the exterior of the van whilst along one side, in huge letters, is the word LOVE. The style, shape and colour of this word is oh so very familiar to me since the brief time I spent in the company of the young sculptor.

'What are we going to do?' asks Tom.

'Well there's not much we can do until we've spent the two million pound donation. Until that time this work of art will need to stay where it is. You never know, we might even replace it with a statue of the old fella.'

When I arrive back at outside my office after the meeting with Tom on the playing fields, I hear my phone mooing. Quickly, I try to push past the Manchester United four-legged centre forward just in time to grab the receiver.

'It's your wife on the phone, Mr Pike,' says Jackie.

I ask her to put Val through. I'm apprehensive as to what she may say having not seen her since before I trashed yet another Mini on our drive.

'Hello, Robert,' she says.

'Hello, Val,' I reply.

'How are you, Robert?'

'Oh, I'm fine, Val and you?'

'Not so bad, not so bad.'

'Good. Did you...'

'Robert, I was wondering...'

'Yes?'

'I was wondering if we could try again?'

These words are music to my ears. Ever since that shambolic night with that vile creature Juanita, I've thought my marriage to Val was well and truly over.'

'I hope we can, my darling,' I reply. 'Come home, please.'

'I am already at home, Robert,' she answers and it feels good to be back. Now all I want is for us to be happy.'

An hour later and I'm driving, carefully, home for what I hope is a happy and lasting reunion with the woman I love.

There is no car on the drive to stand in the way of the BMW, though I'm unsurprised by this as Val's vehicle is most likely in the garage for repair or the breaker's yard. I pull to a stop and get out of the car.

Once inside the house I look around downstairs and through the kitchen window to the garden, but I see no sign of Val. I begin to feel disappointed and wonder if she's had second thoughts when I hear someone descending the stairs.

'Hello Robert,' says Val as we meet in the living room. 'I thought I'd surprise you.'

She most certainly has. She's wearing the same seductive underwear she was displaying on the day I unwittingly exposed myself to her friend Monica so many weeks ago.

'Oh Val, you look wonderful.'

'Then perhaps we can go upstairs and you can show me how wonderful I am.'

I need no other invitation.

CHAPTER 16

TATTOOS, TRAITORS AND TECHNICIANS

"When angry, count to four. When very angry, swear."
Mark Twain

'What do you mean he did it to you while you were asleep?' asks Val, 'And in our own bedroom!'

'I told you. I woke up and there he was, on the bed, doing it.'

'Well why, for heaven's sake, didn't you tell him to stop?'

'I could hardly stop him before he'd finished could I? That would have been even worse.'

'It's disgusting, Robert. How can you even stand the thought of it?' she asks, her face a picture of revulsion.

'My god Val, it's only a bloody tattoo. It's not the end of the world is it? Besides, everyone seems to be having them now.'

In my haste to remove my clothes following Val's seductive request to migrate to the bedroom, I have forgotten to warn her about my newly acquired body art. I've tried to explain how I woke up to find my buttock being used as the Austrian artist's latest canvas and how I had endured excruciating pain in enabling him to finish; the last thing I wanted was a half complete tattoo of the word LOVE splattered across my rear.

Val's discovery of my well kept secret and my embarrassing explanation has rather cooled our ardour.

'Can't you sue him for assault?' asks my wife.

'Oh certainly, on the grounds that I woke up to find a big naked Austrian in my bed slapping Vaseline all over my rear? I think not dear.'

'Well can you have it removed?'

'Listen Val, it nearly bloody killed me having the thing put on. The thought that it might be even more painful having it removed is hardly an incentive.'

'But it's revolting, Robert. I'm not certain I even want to look at it again.'

For one brief moment the sneer of disgust on her face reminds me of the vulture that sits in the Headteacher's office and her distaste for my very existence.

'Well don't look at it,' I snap. 'It's hardly a part of my anatomy you've bothered much about in the past.'

I suppose Val's reaction is understandable. At least now she knows. The most important thing is we are back together, even though we didn't consummate our reunion with an evening of unbridled passion. She'll probably get used to the thing. I'm certainly very much attached and besides, how many people get to be a living, walking, talking work of art? I'll just need to be very careful in the future regarding when and where I remove my trousers.

It's Thursday morning and, like most Thursday mornings, it's the time I walk the corridors to keep myself up to date with what's happening around the place.

Sometimes, if I'm feeling in a particularly masochistic mood, I may even pop in to a lesson or two and speak with the teacher or, heaven forbid, the pupils. Today however, I feel like just walking the school with no interruptions.

Now that we have our new sculptures around it is very easy to navigate the school using the different cows as reference points. Today I start at the ManU cow and head for the Elvis cow, located outside the music department. The impressive volcano cow and imaginative castle cow tells me I am close to the geography and history areas. From there I pass the Barack Obama cow, before turning left at the least imaginatively decorated cow: the cow cow. Moving on, I walk past the staffroom and the marijuana cow sited nearby towards the Argos catalogue cow and then on to the Salvador Dali influenced cow, the pride and joy of the art department. At the end of the long, straight corridor I pass the Laurel and Hardy cow, the Che Guevara cow and the Roald Amunsen cow. It's only as I approach the Headteacher's office I realise something is terribly wrong. The Katherine Lowbridge Headteacher cow has disappeared and in its place stands a ridiculous looking Tom Cruise cow. This calls for action.

'I've had it removed,' says Lowbridge in response to my question as to the whereabouts of the original sculpture.

'You've got no right to have it removed,' I reply. 'It was the work of the children and you can't have it removed just because you don't like the design. That's censorship, it's dictatorial.'

'Whoever said that schools are democracies?' she retorts. 'I will not be humiliated in that way.'

With delight I realise she has handed me an opportunity for merriment; I cannot let it pass.

'Humiliated? Are you saying you think the big cow with a brush stuck to its head was meant to be you?'

She stops and stares at me. Just like the great dragon in my dreams she gives the impression she would like to turn me into a smouldering husk if she could. Purposefully she rises from her chair and points a finger at her door.

'Get out of here. Get out now before I lose my patience. You are nothing but a lazy, contemptuous, trouble making man and one day I'll be rid of you; you mark my words. Now get out!'

There are not many things I find more satisfying than getting the Head Lady to completely fly off the handle. Hopefully one day I will find a way of making her blow a gasket or do something she may live to regret. Maybe if I could track down the missing sculpture and have it located back outside her office I might achieve success in pushing her over the edge. Some investigation is called for.

'I've got no idea, Bob,' says Tom Lavender in answer to the question of the missing Head cow. 'I know it's disappeared, but none of my team moved it and I haven't got the foggiest idea where it could be. Perhaps you should ask Carole.'

Carole is one of the few people in this school that I trust. She is one of those people who somehow manage to get to know everything about everybody. Not only is she the best informed member of staff, but she also holds one of the most powerful roles in the school: she is a technician. Not just any technician, but a fully skilled woodworking, metal bashing, problem solving, resourceful, king daddy of a technician. Best of all, she likes me; a rare characteristic for any woman these days. She has helped me out of many a sticky situation in the past. She is Q to my Bond, Brains to my Jeff, Igor to my Victor. She is wisdom personified, calmness exemplified and she's my best hope in solving the mystery of the disappearing Lowbridge cow.

I arrive at the technician's room and tap out the secret knock. I am only one of very few staff to know this code and feel highly honoured that she shared it with me; without it I would never gain entry in to the inner sanctum.

'Come in.' I hear her voice rumble like distant thunder over the horizon. 'This better be very important or you'll get a try-square rammed up your arse, whoever you are!'

I know she'd make good her threat, too, if she wanted to. I once witnessed the near castration of a young male member of staff who had the temerity to send a child to her asking if she could mend the pupil's broken ruler. Not only did the member of staff spend a painful night in hospital, but the ruler was never seen again.

With great respect I open the door and enter.

'It's me, Bob Pike,' I say quickly, just in case I am mistaken for a burglar or a sex maniac or, even worse, an OFSTED inspector.

'Bob. Come in, it's good to see you,' I hear her say as she emerges from the metal heat treatment room wearing her leather blacksmiths apron, her welding mask, her steel toe-capped Doc Martins and a bikini. 'How are you, stranger?'

She pulls off the mask and strides over to greet me, wrapping her powerful arms around me and squeezing me in a mighty bear hug.

'You old bugger, it's been ages since I've seen you. You don't come down here often enough.'

Without hesitating she releases me from her formidable grip, takes off the apron and slings it over a hook on the door and then picks up a towel from the back of a chair. She starts to wipe herself down.

'Sorry about this, Bob, but I've been welding and casting all morning. I'm sweating like a pig.'

Once she has finished drying off Carole grabs her white coat and puts it on over her bikini. She does all this without batting an eyelid, as though wearing one's swimwear to work is the most natural thing in the world. Maybe it is; maybe all technicians wear such undergarments. I stop myself from pondering on this further, afraid of where it might take me.

'So what's the purpose of the visit, Bob?' she asks as she opens the fridge and takes out a can of ice cold beer. 'Would you like one?'

'No thanks,' I reply, 'not before break.'

She sits down on her favourite chair, one she made herself from the remnants of an old school minibus, and takes a long, thirsty gulp of the beer. She belches loudly as I ask my question.

'I was wondering if you knew about the missing sculpture from outside the Head's office?'

'You mean the one decorated to look like her?' she replies.

'That's the one.'

'I don't know exactly where it is, but I do know that little weasel Ken Grayman had a hand in it. Apparently he went sniffing around Lowbridge and said he could get rid of it for her.'

'Ken Grayman? The traitor.'

'He's your man, Bob,' she answers confidently. 'One other thing, not connected, but could be important.'

When Carole talks like this I'm all ears. Her knowledge is not only remarkable but totally trustworthy.

'There's some new little Spanish tart going around trying to lay down poison about you. She was hooked up with that toad Marriott for a while, but that's all over now; seems like he got cold feet and told her to piss off.'

'Thanks Carole. That could be very useful information,' I answer honestly. 'I can't thank you enough.'

'If you like, I could put some pressure on the bitch,' she says as she picks up a piece of two by one and snaps it in half as if it were a match. 'She'd never cause you any trouble again.'

'Thanks for the offer Carole, you really are a good friend, but I'll pass for the moment. I can handle her.'

As I leave Carole's workplace I reflect on how close to extinction little Juanita had just come.

Ken Grayman is sitting filling out his football pools coupon when I burst into his office.

'Where is it?'

'Bob, what's wrong? You look a bit upset,' he stutters; a characteristic he exhibits when placed under pressure.

'Where's the Lowbridge cow?' I demand. 'I know it was you, you sycophantic little creep. I know you went sucking up to Her Ladyship and said you'd remove it. So where's it gone?'

'I don't know what you're talking about,' he replies as a feeble form of defense.

I stop, take my watch off and stand there looking at the dial.

'I'm going to give you thirty seconds to tell me where it is and if you don't, I'm going to do two things. First, I'm going to call your dear sweet lady wife and tell her you've been shagging Liz Bellamy from drama for the last three years and then I'm going to tell Lowbridge you've been running a little bookmaking service for a number of staff in the school.'

'You wouldn't dare,' he whimpers.

'Twenty-five, twenty-four, twenty-three, twenty-two, twenty one…'

'My wife wouldn't believe you. She knows what a lying, cheating, bastard you are.'

'That's good, but does she also know I've got a photograph of you practising push-ups on top of poor Mrs Bellamy in the drama stockroom?'

'You haven't. I don't believe you,' he answers, his nerves making him stutter.

'Well maybe you're right, but then again, are you prepared to take the gamble? You are, after all, a gambling man. Are you prepared for Mr Bellamy when he arrives at your front door with a baseball bat? I believe that he's quite a big bloke and prone to acts of mindless violence.'

'Why do you need to know? Why is it so important to you? It's only a stupid concrete cow.'

'It might be only a stupid cow to you, but to me it's the lost Ark of the Covenant and the Holy Grail all wrapped up in one; now where is it? Fifteen, fourteen, thirteen, twelve, eleven, ten, nine... '

'Okay, I'll tell you!' he screams. 'But you must promise not to tell Kaz Lowbridge I let on.'

'I won't tell her,' I agree, knowing full well I'll drop him good and deep in the quagmire at the first possible opportunity.

'I gave it to Derek Forrest,' he replies.

'What did you give it him for?'

'To practise with.'

'To practise?' I ask, now totally bemused.

'To practise firing that bloody great catapult of his.'

I lie in bed and reflect on the events of the day. The words of the old woman in the hotel room come tumbling back to me:

"One who is dead will give you much and one that lives will seek to take much from you. A loved one will return and you shall know boundless pleasure, free from the shackles that have kept your lust at bay."

The prophecy seems to be coming true. Old Bill has given me much, at least to administer. Ken Grayman has taken much from me, if I interpret that to mean the Lowbridge cow, and a loved one has returned in the shape of my wife who is lying beside me sleeping peacefully. The boundless pleasures and the removal of shackles to release my lust (without doubt the best part of the prediction) should happen quite soon, then. I do hope so!

Before long I am asleep and dreaming of those boundless pleasures all of which, strangely enough, involve a tall blonde Swedish girl.

CHAPTER 17

RETRIBUTION OF THE WICKED
AND SWEDISH ANGELS

*"A captain who, from private motives, employs his vessel
for another purpose from that intended by the owners, is
answerable to the charge of usurpation, and his crew is
morally and legally entitled to employ forceful means in
wresting his command from him."*
Starbuck:Moby Dick

'She's done what?' I ask Gino Colletti, as he sits in my
office wiping floods of tears from his eyes.

'She was such a wonderful woman and she help me so
much when I come to this school. She say to me, "Gino I
help you with anything you want." She say, "I help you
with your English, I help you with the children." She was
such a lovely person and now she's gone,' he says before
he once more breaks down into fits of uncontrollable
sobbing.

Gino came to me first thing this morning and told me
the unbelievable news: Shirley Makepeace, the most
professional, knowledgeable, reliable, kind, caring,

supportive member of staff has been suspended by Lowbridge and now awaits a Governors' hearing with the possible result of dismissal. The news is almost too incredible to believe, but Gino is a very close friend of Shirley's and he is not the type to create such a fanciful story.

It takes me just one minute to corroborate the facts of the case. I phone Linda Hewlett, and ask her.

'So it's true,' I say as I replace the receiver.

'Yes, yes, I tell you it true, Mr Pike,' says Gino. 'I could strangle that woman with my bare hands for what she do to my Shirley. It not fair. It not right!'

I, of course, totally agree with the highly distraught ex-circus performer and I promise to do what I can to help. He thanks me profusely for the support I promise and leaves my office happier than when he came in. My first task is to go and see Lowbridge and find the answers to several questions, one of which is: why, as her deputy, was I not informed?

'There was no need to involve you,' says Lowbridge calmly. 'This is a matter between Mrs Makepeace, the Governors and me.'

'But we're talking about Shirley,' I protest. 'She's the best damn member of staff we have.'

'That's your opinion,' she sneers. 'I, on the other hand, am not so taken with her, especially in the light of recent performance.'

'So tell me what she has done? I'm your deputy and I should know. How can I field the questions staff are bound to come to me and ask?'

There is a short pause as she mulls over my point.

'Very well,' she eventually replies and gives me the facts.

I may well be a conniving, self-centred, selfish, power hungry, lazy xenophobe, but I still possess a sense of justice, especially when I see one member of staff destroyed as a precursor to my own head being placed upon the block. In addition, my own ego suggests that the only reason Lowbridge went after Shirley was because she felt it would hurt me; a point in which she may well have succeeded. I hate the thought of any type of bullying, that is, unless it's me doing it, in which case I like to think of it not as bullying but more of justifiable intimidation. Lowbridge has made bullying into a new art form; she seems to thrive on it.

These are the thoughts zooming around inside my head as I stomp angrily back to my room to formulate a plan of action. I don't even notice Toby Marriott walking towards me until I almost collide with him; immediately he is on the defensive.

'Listen Bob, I know she's caused you problems, but whatever she tells you, it was all her idea. I want nothing more to do with her. She's bad news in my book,' he babbles.

My mind, however, is focused too heavily on other matters to waste my time discussing his short lived relationship with that poisonous Spanish dwarf. All I manage in reply is a savage, snarling grunt and a look that would peel paint. Screw Marriott and screw Cortez, but most of all screw that vile creation sitting in her palatial office trying to ruin the lives of decent hardworking people or, more to the point, mine.

By the time I reach my office, I've worked myself up into such a temper I fail to remember how difficult it is to get past Wayne Mooney and, as a result, end up with a concrete cow horn jabbed in my groin. I can still feel the pain when, five minutes later, I pick up my phone and dial Shirley Makepeace's home number. In truth, we've never been friends as such, but I have always respected her work and the affection she gives the children.

'Hi Shirley. It's Bob Pike here. I've just heard the news. I was wondering if I could pop round this evening and have a chat.'

It's about six o'clock when I pull up outside the Makepeace residence. Shirley answers the door and straight away I can see she's been crying for many an hour. Her face is red and blotchy and her usually bright eyes are bloodshot and surrounded by a purple puffiness.

'I'm so sorry to hear what has happened, Shirley,' I say as I sit down in the living room.

'She's a vindictive bitch and she's just made all this up to get at me because she thinks I humiliated her in front of the pupils.'

'She says you've been saying things about her to the kids,' I repeat what Lowbridge has told me.

'She's a damn liar,' spits Shirley.

'Apparently there are witnesses.'

'Ken Grayman, Glenys Cooper and that simpleton, William Anthony. They're not witnesses, they're pre-prepared bloody lackeys who'd say anything they were told just to get in her good books.'

'You mean she got them to lie for her?'

'Don't sound so surprised. She wouldn't be the first Headteacher to concoct a story just to get rid of a nuisance member of staff, would she?'

'Point taken,' I reply, hoping she doesn't remind me of some of my little schemes and plots. 'So tell me what really happened to cause this mess.'

Shirley then goes on to give me a full account of the events that led up to her suspension. Apparently, on Monday Lowbridge had arranged to speak to years 9 and 8 to allow her to explain some new fangled initiative she was hoping to introduce into the school next year. Shirley, being the true professional that she is, warned the Headteacher that this might not be the wisest of moves, as putting the whole of year 9 in the same space as the whole of year 8 would be a recipe for disaster; these two year groups are legendary in their collective capacity to bring mayhem to any event.

Lowbridge took this warning to be a slight against her ability to handle large groups of children and admonished Shirley accordingly (yet another case of her shooting the messenger). She said she had no worries and that the children would respect her authority and remain silent throughout; they, of course, did not.

What ensued in the hall that morning turned out to be nothing short of carnage and, according to Shirley, the Headteacher was lucky to escape without any physical scars. In the end Lowbridge's lack of control forced Shirley to step in and bring the children to some kind of order. Without her intervention things could have turned nasty, but Lowbridge did not view it this way after the event. Instead, with her massive ego dented and her pride bashed, she held Shirley responsible for humiliating her in front of the pupils.

After that, probably because she was haunted by the shame, Lowbridge set about concocting a story whereby she could prove Shirley was systematically undermining her authority by telling the children damaging things about her. She had even conjured up several "reliable" members of staff to act as witnesses.

'Even my Union has told me that the facts are pretty damning, and you can bet your life she will be working on others, including kids, to back up her story,' says Shirley as she finishes recounting the sorry tale. 'What am I going to do, Bob? I'm just glad Maurice isn't here to witness this crap.'

Maurice, Shirley's husband, died twelve months ago, after a long battle with cancer. She had been very brave throughout and, in order to cope with the sorrow of her tragic loss, had thrown herself in to her work.

I drive away from the house having promised I will do all I can and maybe, for once, I am sincere in my pledge.

I arrive home much later than usual and I'm pleased to see the insurance company have finally enabled Val to pick up her new, blue Mini Cooper. It sits there on the drive all sparkling and pristine.

Inside the house I find Val busy preparing a meal and the table laid with all the trimmings, including candles.

'Hello darling,' she says buoyantly, when she sees me. 'You're slightly later than I thought you'd be but I've kept everything warm so you can sit down, relax and enjoy a wonderful, romantic dinner.'

Val has always had a real gift for creating an occasion at short notice. This evening illustrates that talent perfectly. We eat, drink and talk. I tell her about my problems and she lends a sympathetic ear. The more the evening progresses the more I regret lusting after another woman and the more I realise how much I love the lady sitting opposite me.

'She deserves to have something really horrible happen to her,' she says, in way of comment on Lowbridge's bully-boy approach to leadership.

After the sumptuous meal more wine flows, followed by coffee and Cognac. After this, it seems only right to open more wine. Whenever she consumes large amounts of wine Val always becomes more and more talkative; this occasion is no exception, especially as we are discussing such an emotive subject.

'She's a total bitch by the sound of it,' says a fairly squiffy Val. 'I don't know how you put up with her.'

Her glass is empty and she holds it out waiting for a refill before she continues. I pour her another glass and top-up my own.

'She'll get her comeuppance, you mark my words. People like her don't survive forever, and then you can take over. You'd be a thousand times better than her as Headteacher,' she says and then takes a very large gulp of the red. 'Even Toby says you would.'

The comment has the instant effect of stopping the conversation. I place my glass on the table whilst she avoids my stare and takes another sip of her drink.

'Toby? Toby Marriott? When have you spoken to him?'

'Oh, I, er, bumped into him on the high street the other day.'

She's lying. I've known her too long and she has always been terrible at concocting untruths, however, this is not the time to bring her honesty in to question.

'Oh really,' I answer, picking up my glass again and acting as naturally as possible. 'That's very kind of him to say so.'

I make sure that the rest of the evening passes without another hitch by changing the subject and we talk about everything from the theatre to holidays; I don't want this evening to be spoiled.

Eventually the alcohol begins to make Val very tired and she craves the comfort of her bed. Playing the perfect gentleman, I escort her to the bedroom and see she is tucked in before I return downstairs to, as I tell her, tidy a few things away. This is no more than a ploy, for what I really want to do is a little bit of investigation.

My wife is a creature of habit and always leaves her mobile phone on a small occasional table next to the sofa in the lounge. Yes, there it is, waiting for me to begin my sleuthing.

As I suspected, she has not deleted her old text messages and, as I scroll through them, I see Toby's name appearing again and again and again. I open one of the messages.

"C u at 8" is all it says; incriminating enough, but not conclusive.

I switch to the "sent messages" folder and here I find the evidence I need to back up my suspicions.

"I had a gr8 nite. I'll miss u till I c u again" was sent as recently as three weeks ago.

I scroll back even further.

"I've bought some new underwear especially 4 u. Can't wait for you 2 find it" says one of the earliest messages, the date places it at the time I rudely interrupted her lingerie party with Monica.

She's been seeing him for months, even before the time when things began to turn sour between us. All the times she said she was going to the gym, or yoga classes, or her Spanish night school she was actually seeing him.

I stand retracing the past months in my mind. Toby's words of earlier in the day come flooding back to me.

'Listen, Bob, I know she's caused you problems, but whatever she tells you, it was all her idea. I want nothing more to do with her; she's bad news in my book.'

I lie in bed; Val is solidly asleep next to me. Sleep soon comes for me and I dream I am sitting on a simple chair in an empty room with no windows or doors. No one visits me in my room and the walls are too thick for me to break out, which is good because I like my room. My room is uncomplicated and clean and I want no one to spoil it. A small voice starts to talk to me. The more it says the more I am forced to listen and the more I listen the louder it gets and as it gets louder I am compelled to give it a physical form.

I know who she is even before she appears. It was the same voice that guided me to help Daniel Webster, to save Toby Marriott and aid Derek Forrest with his ludicrous scheme. She is the sea nymph of my dreams, the old woman prophet I saw in the hotel room and the Swedish beauty I found in the same room the next morning. She has been with me for years and speaks to me regularly. She is my guardian, she is my angel.

'I love you, Robert,' she says, as she kisses me on the cheek. 'I'm the only one that loves you.'

She is the most beautiful woman I have ever seen, but her physical form is always changing and I find it difficult to keep her image in my mind. She is a pure blonde and then a redhead. Her hair changes to jet black and her skin becomes the colour of ebony, then milk white and then golden. She is tall and slender and then tiny and petite. Her eyes change colour with every second that I stare at her.

'What is your name?' I ask.

'I am whoever you want me to be,' she replies. 'I will always be faithful and I will always be with you.'

'Why have you come to my room?'

'I have come to release you,' she replies and she sits on my lap and begins to stroke my hair.

'But I am happy here in my room,' I reply. 'Why should I want to escape? Why should I want to leave it?'

'You must, because the time has come for you to fulfill your destiny. Greatness planned for you.'

'What greatness?' I ask, intrigued.

'I cannot tell you. I cannot show you until you are free of these walls and these shackles.'

As she says this I look down and see that I am bound to the chair by coils and coils of thick, steel chain.

'How can I remove these?' I ask. 'I am not strong enough.'

'But I am,' she replies, smiling sweetly and then brushes her soft lips against mine.

The nearness of her body makes me eager to reach out and touch her, but my hands are held firm by the chains.

She kisses me more passionately and I struggle to free myself.

'They are too strong!' I shout. 'Help me.'

'Very well,' she answers, and jumps from my lap.

She begins to grow until she fills the room and then she grabs my chains and snaps them with ease. I stand, free to walk around my room for the first time.

'What about the walls?' booms the beautiful girl, now a giant.

'Smash them down,' I instruct her. 'Destroy them. Turn them to rubble!'

She grows even bigger and presses her arms against the ceiling and the walls. With great effort she starts to crack the masonry. Eventually she forces herself to stand and the room disintegrates. The beautiful woman vanishes.

I am alone again, but this time I stand on a long road leading to the horizon that glitters with a golden light.

'What do I do now?' I ask the nothingness.

'Follow the road,' says her voice.

'Where am I going?'

'Wherever you want to, Robert.'

I start walking.

CHAPTER 18

PLANS, TRAPS AND AUTOMOBILES

"Watch your thoughts, for they become words.
Watch your words, for they become actions.
Watch your actions, for they become habits.
Watch your habits, for they become character.
Watch your character, for it becomes your destiny."
Unknown

At the Senior Leadership meeting yesterday evening I found out that Shirley Makepeace has been officially dismissed by the Governors. When Lowbridge told us she tried to sound upset but I am sure I caught a small smirk on her face when she glibly said:

'The Governors were left with no choice but to dismiss Mrs Makepeace, forthwith.'

The sniffling, wretched excuses of humanity, or rather the three other members of the team, nodded their heads somberly. William Anthony even had the temerity to compliment Lowbridge on her bravery in carrying out such a difficult task.

All through the meeting she kept her eyes on me as though she was waiting for me to argue against the decision. I was prepared for this and remained stony-faced for the duration of the whole meeting and left without saying a word to anyone. I did not sleep well, as thinking about Shirley and my promise to help kept my mind active. I arrived at school this morning not in the best frame of mind.

'I'm sorry Gino, can you repeat that.'

I stare at the phone receiver in my hand, not believing what I have just heard.

'She die! Shirley, she die, she killed herself.'

After this phone call from a distraught Gino it takes me a couple of hours to find out the facts as to what happened.

Evidently, yesterday evening at approximately the same time as Lowbridge was delivering her statement, Shirley Makepeace was tying a length of chord around a girder in her garage. She was found dead, having hanged herself, early in the morning after neighbours complained to police that her dogs had been barking for several hours.

Following this news I walk the corridors in an almost stunned trance. Everywhere I go I hear staff talking about the tragedy; the news has travelled at lightening speed.

Several members of staff stop me and shake their heads in disbelief and then find they are too upset to say anything. As yet the pupils know nothing, but it won't be long before they do, and when the news is made public there will be a lot of very upset children to cope with. Shirley was the most popular member of staff with the pupils.

My walkabout eventually leads me to the Tom Cruise cow and the door marked 'Headteacher'. I knock and enter without waiting for permission.

Lowbridge is in there, as are the three Assistant Toadies.

'You've heard the news then?' I ask, not caring if I'd interrupted anything important.

'What news would that be?' replies Lowbridge.

'Don't be pathetic. You know very well what news I'm talking about,' I snap. 'I was wondering if you'd heard that the year 10 football team won their cup match last night?'

'Mr Pike, I think you are a little upset, but that does not excuse the fact that you are out of order,' she replies in her smarmiest, slimiest voice. 'Perhaps you should come back later.'

'Why later? Aren't you having a management meeting now?' I answer, indicating Sycophants United sitting on three chairs opposite her.

'We were just discussing next year's timetable,' she lies in reply.

'Oh good, I hope you all have a wonderful time. It's a pity Shirley isn't here to talk about it too. Still, at least one good thing has come out of this,' I spit at them. 'You've made a heck of a saving on the wage bill for next year.'

With that I leave, making certain the door rattles its frame and threatens to snap its hinges.

My attitude and insubordination will have got right up her nose, especially as this time I had an audience. I've had enough of her games; I've had enough of her intimidation, her bullying and enough of her! More than ever I want to destroy her and more than ever I plan to try.

I decide to get some fresh air and head for the nearest exit that leads to the school playing fields. I'm just through the doors when I hear my name called.

'Bob, Bob!' shouts Tom Lavender as he comes running up behind me. 'Hi Bob, tragic news about poor Shirley isn't it?'

Ever since the inheritance left to him by Old Bill Trundell, the site manager has radically changed. He comes to work driving a brand new Aston Martin and wears Armani suits. However, his personal body odour has not moved one notch on the sniffometer and rather than face him directly I shift position slightly in order that I may breathe freely and reduce the risk of gagging or vomiting.

'Terribly tragic,' I agree.

'Terrible I know, but that's not the reason I want to talk to you,' he replies. 'I know it's not a good time, but I want to complain about two members of staff.'

'Go on,' I answer.

'I know I should really tell the Head, but I don't want to get them into too much trouble and I know what Ms Lowbridge is like.'

'I understand, Tom, so tell me and I'll be discreet.'

'It's Mr Marriott and that new Spanish teacher.'

I'm all ears.

'What have they been up to?'

'Well, they keep going in Old Bill's caravan and using it.'

'What do you mean, using it?'

'I think they're going in there and doing things.'

'Ah, I see,' I reply. 'When are they using it exactly?'

'Anytime they can,' he answers, scratching the back of his head. 'Before school, after school, break times, lunch times and, occasionally, during lesson times.'

'That's awful,' I reply in mock horror. 'You've done the best thing in speaking to me about this, Tom. Leave it with me and I'll handle it. Don't worry, no one will get in to trouble and I won't implicate you, okay?'

Tom Lavender thanks me profusely before jogging back to his den, content that he has off-loaded his heavy burden.

I spend the rest of the day in the library as this room has the best view over the playing fields. Just as Tom said, Marriott and the Spanish harlot are regular visitors to the old caravan. Will I do anything about it, as promised? Of course I will, but all in my own good time.

Following my vigil in the library I seek out Gino Colletti. I find him after school in the gym, hanging upside down from the top wall bar.

'Hello Gino, can I talk to you for a moment?'

For several moments there is not a single movement or acknowledgement of my presence. Then suddenly he bursts out of his chrysalis state, grabs hold of the bar, flips his body to an upright position and launches himself into the air. My breath catches in my throat as he twists and gyrates in mid air and then eventually lands as light as a feather on the balls of his feet with arms outstretched to provide balance.

'Hello Mr Pike,' he says as he grabs my hand and shakes it violently.

'Hello Gino,' I reply. 'How are you bearing up?'

'I am very sad, Mr Pike,' he says, his eyes full of sorrow. 'Shirley was a wonderful person. She did not deserve what happens, but she told me a few days ago that

177

you had tried to help and so I, Gino Colletti, thanks you from the bottom of my heart.'

'And how do you feel about Ms Lowbridge these days?' I ask.

His eyes narrow and his lips curl. I see the veins in his powerful neck start to bulge with an influx of blood.

'I would like to take her neck in my bare hands and squeeze it until I hear it break,' he says with total venom.

I place a calming hand on his shoulder.

'But that wouldn't be a good idea would it?' I say. 'Shirley would not want you to get into trouble.'

He nods his head, agreeing with everything I've said.

'You are right, Mr Pike.'

'That doesn't mean she should get away with what she has done, though, does it?'

His eyes widen.

'I do not understand.'

'I mean, there are other ways in which we can punish her for what she did to poor Shirley.'

'Ah yes, now I understand,' he smiles. 'In my old country we have a word vendetta; it means that if someone does something bad to you, you will do something bad to them.'

'Well then, how would you like to carry out a little vendetta against Ms Lowbridge?'

'I will help you any way I can, Mr Pike.'

'Good, I thought you might.'

Back at home Val is preparing to go to her yoga class.

'I've left a lasagne in the oven for you, honey,' she says and then kisses me on the cheek 'I'll see you about ten-thirty.'

I acknowledge what she has said and wave her off from the front doorstep. When she is out of sight I go into the kitchen to find the food she has prepared. I serve myself a decent portion. As usual the meal is excellent; I almost enjoy eating it. When I've finished I load the dishwasher, change into more casual clothes and go out to my car.

The drive to the community centre where Val goes for her yoga classes only takes about fifteen minutes. I pull on to the car park and get out, looking for her car as I do so; it's not there. I go in to the centre and look through the small window in the door of the hall where the class is scheduled. There are about fifteen people in the group; Valerie is not one of them. Next, I get back in the BMW and drive across town to where Toby Marriott has his apartment. The blue Mini Cooper is parked down a side road close to Marriott's address.

Satisfied with the night's work I drive back home. On the way I call in at the club, hoping to find a friend there; I'm not disappointed.

'Hello Colin. How are things?'

Colin is in his usual position: sitting on a stool at the end of the bar.

'Hi, Bob,' he replies, although he looks less than happy to see me.

He has never quite recovered from the bashing his teeth had from my golf ball. I think he has always thought I planned the shot on purpose. Still, the poor bloke did get put through the mill.

'How's the old mouth feeling?' I can't resist asking him.

'It still hurts like buggery, if you really want to know.'

'I bet it does. Still, I'm sure you'll get it sorted out soon,' I reply smugly. 'Tell me Colin, is Monica still selling that range of lingerie?'

'The Erotica line? Yes, she's doing quite well with it, why?'

'I want to buy some as a gift for Val and was wondering if you could ask Monica to give me a call.'

'Yeah, I'll tell her when I get home.'

'Don't forget to tell her it's a secret,' I remind him before I leave. 'I want it as a surprise for Val. I'm planning a weekend away for the pair of us.'

I've been back at home for at least half an hour when Val arrives back. I'm sitting up in bed reading when she breezes into the room.

'Oh, you're in bed,' she says, sounding mildly surprised. 'I think I'll join you after I've had a shower. I'm all hot and sweaty after the hard work in class.'

'I bet you are,' I reply.

By the time she's finished her shower I have put my book away and turned off my light. I pretend to be asleep when she gets into bed. It doesn't take her long to fall asleep, no doubt exhausted by her exertions earlier in the evening.

It's obvious now that Toby finished with Val and thought she was about to confess the affair to me, so he came to me first. She didn't confess though, probably because she hoped he would change his mind; it appears he has.

I'm exhausted. Sleep should come easily, but it doesn't; my mind is too active. I do not sleep and I do not dream.

Instead, I plan how I can set my traps and all the time in my head a little voice keeps me company.

CHAPTER 19

RHAPSODY IN BLACK AND A CHANGE OF NAME

"To be prepared is half the victory."
Miguel de Cervantes

This is the second colleague whose funeral I have attended this year. To be able to attribute the cause of both deaths to the Headteacher of the school they work for must be unique.

Whilst the number of people who turned out for Old Bill's funeral was more than I'd expected, the number who congregate in memoriam for Shirley Makepeace is phenomenal, though no more than I would have predicted. She was well liked and very popular. For her to feel such despair that she thought the only way out was to take her own life is tragic. News that she was dismissed from the school hours before her suicide is now common knowledge and the whole sad, sorry affair has polarized the opinion of the staff and students. Lowbridge's personal exchange rate, never high at the best of times, has plummeted to rock bottom over the last few days. It is a terrible thought to have at this time but I can't help thinking that recent events will aid my course of action over the days to come.

I have been instructed by Lowbridge to represent the school on her behalf, the reasons for this being obvious. There are also some other noticeable absentees. The Gang of Three treacherous Assistant Headteachers has not made the journey to the cemetery and neither have the majority of the Governors. I'm not surprised considering the part they all played in pushing Shirley over the edge.

Shirley had only a few living relatives and most of these live too far away to make the journey. At the request of the one family member able to join the congregation, an elderly cousin from High Wycombe, I am making a speech on behalf of the school.

'I knew Shirley as a friend and a colleague for over fifteen years. In all this time I found her to be the most gifted and professional teacher I have ever had the pleasure to know. There are many colleagues here today who have benefited from her wisdom and kind support,' I say, and look down from where I am standing to see a large number of staff, including Gino, weeping, ' but she will probably be best remembered for being a true friend to every pupil in the school. Thousands of pupils have passed through the school whilst Shirley was here and she took time to get to know every one of them. Not only that, but she cared about every one of them and she believed in every one of them.'

I take a short pause and gaze around the congregation. The school council is there, representing the pupils of the school; there's not a dry eye amongst them.

'That's why she will never be forgotten and I will make certain that her name remains forever synonymous with the name of Laburnum High School. I intend to name the new pupil support centre "The Shirley Makepeace Centre" as a lasting memorial to a great person.'

I pause once more, this time to allow the spontaneous round of applause to subside before I continue.

'I feel proud to have worked with such a person. I feel proud to have known such a person and I feel proud to have been her friend.'

Another round of applause and I pause again.

'And now I'd like you all to join me in singing Shirley's favourite song. Mr Stanforth of the music department has kindly agreed to play the piano to accompany Sheryl Greaves and Donna Claxton of Year 8 on recorders.'

From their positions in the congregation the music teacher and his two protégés walk to the front and take up their positions.

'Ladies and gentlemen, would you all stand and join us in singing of Queen's Bohemian Rhapsody.'

'What were you thinking? You can't just start making promises about what you intend to name the new pupil support centre,' shouts Lowbridge as I stand in her office to receive my dressing down, now a regular feature of my life at school.

'It's going to be called the Shirley Makepeace Centre,' I state, ignoring her outburst of rage, 'or I won't release the funds to see that it gets built.'

'You have no right!' she screams. 'I decide what happens in this school. I decide what happens! The Governors will have something to say about this.'

'The Governors. The Governors. Why don't you stop hiding behind the Governors; they only do as you tell them. You don't want Shirley's name on that building because you know you killed her just as the staff know you killed her and the children know you killed her,' I snap back. 'You're not a very popular person at this moment in time.'

She wants to explode; I can see it in her eyes. If she could strike me she would, but she's too wise for that. She is fighting to gain control of herself.

'Get out of my sight,' she says. 'Get out and stay out. I've had about as much as I can take from you. I'm going to finish you; I'm going to destroy you.'

'We'll see,' I reply defiantly, and once again test the strength of the hinges on the door of her office as I leave.

I didn't want a confrontation, but I had no choice once she found out about the funeral service and my announcement. However, what's done is done and there is no going back. She'll definitely try to get me out now and at this minute is probably talking to the Chair. If I am to go through with my plan it will have to be sooner rather than later, I may not have much time left.

After leaving her office I head down towards the technology department to have a word with Derek Forrest. The trebuchet that he and his team of young helpers have been building is complete and ready for the attempt on the record.

'So when do you think you'll go for it?' I ask him.

'Everything is okay. We've been in touch with The Guinness Book of Records people and they're sending some verifiers up to us this Friday. The BBC wants to send a camera crew so we thought after school at four o'clock would be the best time.'

'This Friday? That soon?' I hadn't expected this. My plan has to fit around this deadline. 'Okay Derek, that sounds fine. We'll announce it in the briefing tomorrow morning.'

I leave him to get back to his teaching and head for the P.E department I need to speak to Gino. I find him on the field supervising a football game.

'No, no, hold on to the ball, don't give it away. Treat the ball like a beautiful woman; keep it, caress it, love it…'

'And kick it every now and then,' I say, unable to resist.

'Ah Mr Pike. How are you?' he asks, without taking his eye off the game. 'How can I help you?'

'Are you still interested in the matter we spoke about the other day? If you are we will need to move this Thursday night.'

He drops his concentration from the game of football and turns to face me.

'Are you certain no one will be hurt?'

'No one will be hurt, Gino; as I've told you, we will just be teaching her a lesson.'

'Then you can count me in; I will do it for the memory of my friend Shirley,' he replies, crossing himself as he does so.

'Good, then we will meet at the arranged place at eleven-thirty and remember to bring all your gear.'

'You can count on me, Mr Pike.'

Two parts of the puzzle are in place. Every other aspect is down to me. Next stop, science.

There are very few perks in teaching, even the long holiday argument is wearing thin these days. However, owing to the fact that I am a science teacher I have access to the chemical cabinet and just right now this is a perk. Health and safety officials would have a field day if they made a visit at the moment. Some of the chemicals must have been here years and, quite possibly, are now kept illegally. Take chloroform, for example. It was developed and used mainly as an anesthetic as it depresses the central nervous system, causing dizziness, fatigue and unconsciousness. Why, then, do we keep some in school? Who knows? It does, however, suit my purpose perfectly. There are only two other members of staff that are aware that we have it: Doug Ansoll, the Head of science and the most cynical bastard on the face of the planet, and Judith McLauren, the science technician of some twenty years.

As Deputy Headteacher I have access to every room in the building including the science prep room where all the chemicals and equipment are kept. For most of the day the room is empty, but locked. My master key gets me in and I head straight for the cupboard where, stored right at the back, the glass bottle containing the chloroform is kept. It takes me only seconds and I'm back in the corridor. Because I teach in the department no one takes any notice of me and, with the small bottle tucked securely under my jacket, I make my way back to my office, satisfied that I've successfully completed all the groundwork in school. Now for setting up the other aspects of my plan.

I return home to find Val sitting out in the garden tending her precious rose bushes.

'Hi darling, what are you doing?' I ask her. I'm not in the least bit bothered, but it's best to keep up the pretence, at least for the next two days.

'I'm only dead-heading the roses. I want to make the bushes continue to flower for as long as I can.'

'Good,' I respond.

'It was such a shame he died,' she says as she stands up from her kneeling pad and stretches her limbs. 'He was so gifted in his field.'

'Who was?' I ask, again with no real interest.

'Mister Rose; Old Bill. He was a genius. It was his articles that inspired me to start growing roses. To find out that he worked at your school is truly amazing.'

She begins to pack away her many garden implements into the neat little storage container. When she is satisfied everything is stored in its correct place she takes the box to her potting shed.

I'm back inside having a cold drink when she walks into the kitchen.

'I've prepared you a cold meat salad for this evening, Bob' she says.

'Are you going out?' I enquire innocently.

'Yes,' she replies in a matter-of-fact way. 'Poor Gloria is sick and she's asked if I would prompt at the theatre tonight; you know how much amateurs rely on having their lines at hand.'

After she has left the house I go upstairs, change my clothes and then go outside to my car. I open the boot and check everything once more. The package supplied by Monica is next to the small case containing the chloroform and next to that is the lengths of rope and two torches. Satisfied that I have everything I need I get in the car and head off across town. I find the Mini Cooper parked down the same side road near to Marriott's apartment. Valerie's excursion tonight was unexpected, but it does give me an opportunity to reduce the amount of work I will need to do tomorrow.

I park the BMW a few streets away and walk to where the Mini is parked. Using her spare key I get into the car and drive off. I intend to put the car in the last place Val would expect: our garage. In all the years we have lived at our current address Val has never so much as set foot in it. She says it is my domain, just as the potting shed and the greenhouse are hers.

Once I have the car safely stowed away I phone for a taxi to take me back to my car. In less than one and three quarter hours after first setting off I'm back home. I pour myself a stiff drink and sit and wait for the inevitable phone call.

At eleven-thirty I answer the phone.

'Bob, Bob, someone has stolen my car!'

I can tell she is very upset as her voice is cracking and she has obviously been crying. Good.

'Oh my God, where was it? Stay where you are I'll be right over...'

She interrupts me.

'No Bob, I'm alright really,' she almost shouts. 'I've called a taxi. There's no need for you to come here.'

'Are you certain?' I persist. 'I could be at the theatre in about fifteen minutes.'

'No Bob, in fact the taxi has just arrived; I'll be home soon,' she says and then hangs up.

I feel sorry for Val. On the face of it she is the perfect wife, but perfect wives do not have an affair with a Lothario like Toby Marriott. Perfect wives do not say they are going to their yoga class, only to end up in the sack with a sex-mad little shit, and perfect wives do not rub your nose in the mire over every small marital transgression you have made whilst they are being humped by the local gigolo.

Yes, I feel sorry for Val, but not enough to stop me going through with my plan.

She arrives home in a real state. I ask if she's called the police; she tells me she has. That may or may not be the truth, it really doesn't matter either way.

In sleep I dream I am still walking the straight path towards the golden horizon; it is now much nearer.

CHAPTER 20

THE BAD SAMARITAN AND A DISH
SERVED COLD

"I am the punishment of God...If you had not committed
great sins; God would not have sent a punishment
like me upon you."
Genghis Khan

'Then a Samaritan came walking along and the poor man lying beaten on the floor saw him and knew him to be an enemy of his tribe and thought no help will come from this man. Yet the Samaritan did not walk on by; instead he stopped and went over to the fellow lying beaten and bruised on the ground. He asked the man what had happened and the man said he had been beaten and robbed. Then the Samaritan asked if the man was in pain and the man answered that he was. "I will help you," said the Samaritan and with that he took out his knife and slit the throat of the poor beaten and robbed man and thereby ended his misery, for he was a Good Samaritan.'

I often change some of the details in well-known stories. One of my more creative endings has the

Samaritan, disguised as Rolf Harris, saying: "We'll come back next week and see how the little fella is getting along." It actually makes no difference what I say as no one listens. I can say what I like. Staff and students sit with blank faces and empty minds just waiting for the purgatory of morning assembly to be over so they can carry on with their lives and not have to consider morals and values.

I also dislike being in assembly, but for different reasons. I'm usually the "someone" who is required to stand on the stage preaching to the masses, knowing full that nothing I say will change those who are made to sit in front of me. On most days school assembly is a chore to be got through as quickly as possible so we can tick another little box on the Governments list of requirements. An assembly, no matter how crass, stupid, boring or irrelevant is still a session of collective worship. Job done; tick the box, on to the next task.

Today is different, however. Today I need to use the end of my assembly to good effect as the success of my plan, the plan where I mete out revenge on all those who have hurt me, relies on the notice I am about to give.

'Tomorrow evening,' I begin, changing the tone of my voice so that everyone wakes up. I need as many pupils as possible to take in this information, 'there will be an attempt on a world record. At four o'clock tomorrow afternoon Mr Forrest and his team will fire the trebuchet they have been building. They will try to throw a small car over four hundred metres. You are all invited as, of course, are your parents. Refreshments will be provided. Officials from The Guinness Book of Records will be on hand to record and verify the event and the BBC News are sending a camera team to film the action as it happens. I hope you will all try and attend.'

I repeat the message, just to make certain at least a decent percentage of the throng understand. The assembly ends and the children and staff leave the hall to the strains of Cat Stevens singing *Morning Has Broken.* I, without delay, head for my office.

Gino is waiting for me and I struggle to get past the centre-forward cow to unlock and enter my office. Gino, on the other hand, has no trouble gliding past the great concrete edifice.

'Have you brought it?' I ask as soon as he closes the door behind him.

He nods in the affirmative and takes out the object, neatly wrapped in a football sock that he has tucked into the waistband of his tracksuit bottoms.

'Does anyone know you took it?' I ask. This is the last component I need to successfully execute my plan; nothing must go wrong now.

'No one saw me, Mr Pike,' he confirms 'I very careful.'

I remove the item from the sock and feel the cold, heavy steel in my hand.

'Is it clean?' I question.

'Yes, it very clean; I take it apart and oil it myself.'

'I meant the sock.'

Everything is in place and all I need is a final run through with Gino tonight. Tomorrow the show begins and the additional four unsuspecting players will enter my drama.

That evening I tell Val I'm going to the golf club. She appears pleased with the news and I don't need to guess why. My destination, however, is not the club but a sports centre where I have arranged a clandestine meeting with Gino Colletti to go through his part in my plan. He treats me to a demonstration of his acrobatic skills that fills me with confidence.

I arrive home later than anticipated, having dropped in to the golf club to make my alibi watertight. Val is already curled up and in the land of nod when I climb into bed beside her. She has no idea this will be the longest sleep she has ever had.

Quietly I set my alarm for an hour earlier than usual and settle down for the night. On the floor at the side of the bed next to me sits the small case containing the chloroform and various other bits of apparatus. I am ready to do what I must do tomorrow.

I have reached the end of the path and stand at the base of a huge golden tower. The tower seems to reach to the very stars. Four great dragons fly above me circling the tower, challenging me to climb to its summit. The largest of these beasts wears a dark business suit and has an orange scrubbing brush glue-gunned to the top of its head. The next dragon wears a set of black lingerie, including stockings and suspenders. The other two wear no clothes, but are always entwined, copulating enthusiastically as they soar and swoop in the skies.

From a door at the base of the Golden Tower emerges a beautiful blonde princess with eyes of jade and skin the colour of pure cream.

'If you want me, you know what you must do, my love,' she purrs, the softness of her voice caressing my mind.

'I would do anything to be with you,' I reply, but as I reach out to touch her hand the largest of the dragons swoops down and plucks the maiden from within my grasp.

'I will destroy you,' booms the beast. 'I will kill all hope you have. You are mine.'

'No!' I scream and then begin to climb the tower.

The narrow staircase winds its way around the outside of the structure and, as I climb higher, the dreadful beasts try to attack me and make me lose my footing, but I manage to keep on walking and eventually I come to a small platform. Here I find a golden bow and a quiver of gold and silver arrows. I take up the weapon and draw back an arrow, pointing it at the two copulating monsters.

When I release the arrow it sails straight and true, passing right through one of them to embed itself in the torso of the other. Frantically they flap their wings and stay in flight, but to no avail as they fall and crash to the ground.

Next I fire my bow at the dragon in the erotic underwear and it, too, heads earthbound with an arrow protruding from its side. As it falls it lets out a hideous scream before exploding in a cloud of dust as it impacts with the earth.

Of the four mighty dragons only the big brush-headed giant remains aloft, still clutching my jade-eyed beauty in its vicious claws and booming obscenities at me.

'Fire your bow little man and then watch me squeeze the juice from this little plum,' it shouts, as streaks of red flame fly from its prodigious snout.

Slowly and deliberately I take aim at the place I assume the monster's heart to be, but a small voice tells me to point the arrow to another place and obediently, I comply. With unerring accuracy the arrow leaves the bow and flies straight and true right up the dragon's considerable rectum.

Its scream flattens forests and crumbles mountains. Its scream diverts rivers and empties oceans. Defeated, it sails towards the earth below and as it does it releases the blonde beauty from its claws. The creature ploughs into the ground like a monstrous meteorite, its body splitting open and spilling guts over the land.

The maiden still falls, but I leap from my platform and catch her in my arms before gently coming to rest on the ground.

'What is your name?' I ask the cream-skinned Princess. 'I am Hope,' she replies.

My alarm wakens me and my reflexes are impressive enough not to allow more than one beep to fracture the quiet of the early hours. Carefully, I reach down and open the small case at the side of the bed. From inside I take a small steel gauze cage, a piece of cotton lint and the bottle of precious chloroform. Gently, I ease Val onto her back and hold the lint covered gauze over her nose and mouth. I pull the cork stopper from the bottle, careful not to inhale, and drop five drops of the liquid onto the cotton.

Val's eyes begin to flutter open, but she is unable to fight the effects of the chloroform.

'Go back to sleep, my love,' I whisper. 'I'll wake you later, much later.

She'll sleep for a good six hours before I need to top up the dose and that's all the time I'll need to do what needs to be done.

I get out of bed, shower then get ready for work. After a light breakfast I go and get the Mini from the garage. On the back seat I make a bed for Valerie to lie on. Next I go back upstairs and having dressed her, carry her downstairs and out to the car.

The drive to school is problem free and I park up just behind Old Bill's caravan. It's still very early and when I'm certain no one is around I carry Val out of the car and place her in the bedroom of the caravan; she is still unconscious. Once I have made certain she is comfortable I go back to the Mini and drive it to the staff car park where it will stand until later in the day. I now have time to make myself a coffee in my office before my next deadline.

My watch alarm beeps at seven forty-five. This is my cue to head back to the caravan, this time carrying a roll of gaffer tape, several A3 sheets of paper and my attaché case. Back inside the caravan I check Val's breathing and pulse and then sit on the edge of the bed behind the door and wait. As I wait the doubts start to creep in. What if they don't show? What if someone else turns up?

I should not have worried for at eight o'clock I hear the door to the caravan swing open and two familiar, giggling individuals enter. I've already taken the item supplied by Gino from the case and I'm holding it ready when they enter. Juanita is first into the bedroom, already half undressed, closely followed by Toby Marriott, his trousers around his ankles.

By the time they realise I'm in the room it's too late and I kick the door shut.

'You're on time,' I say calmly, as I raise the hand gun and point it at the pair of them. 'That's very good.'

'Bob, what the bloody hell are you doing?' asks Toby, his eyes not leaving the barrel pointed at his chest.

'Shut up you little shit,' I spit. 'I'll do the talking and you two can listen.'

Juanita has more fire than her lover and starts cursing me in her native tongue. She is quite prepared to charge at me; an action I am prepared for. However, Toby is less than willing to take such a gamble and holds the golden-skinned little firebrand at bay.

On the bed I have placed several pieces of rope ready for the next phase. Toby has seen Val lying comatose on the bed.

'Oh my God, is she dead?'

I ignore his question and instead give him his instruction.

'Tie her up,' I order him, indicating Juanita.

This provokes more abuse, but it's only what I'm prepared for.

'No one can hear us, and no one will care if they could; they'd just think it was you two at it like rabbits again, so save your breath.'

Toby is so scared he can barely carry out his task, but eventually he makes a good fist of securing his little Latin lover. When he's finished I get him to lay Juanita next to my wife.

'Now listen, Bob, I'm sorry about everything. I tried to split from Val, but she kept coming back,' he pleads, but all it gains is a glare in his direction from Juanita.

'You still seeing this bitch?' she spits. 'You told me that was all over.'

'Oh, dear, it seems like you've let the cat out the bag now, dear boy,' I say before indicating he should turn around.

'What are you going to do, Bob? You're not going to do anything rash are you?'

'Put your hands behind your back,' I snap and I slip a pre prepared loop over his hands then lash them securely keeping the pistol pressed hard between his shoulder blades. When his hands are bound I push him roughly onto the bed and slip another loop around his ankles.

'What are you going to do, you mad bastard?' Toby screams frantically as I methodically take the small steel cage covered with the cotton lint and place it over his nose and mouth. I clamp his head firmly under my arm before I take the bottle and allow several drops to be absorbed by the fabric. He fights the effects of the fumes for several seconds, but then I feel him go limp; he is quite unconscious. I remember to get his car keys from his jacket before I move on to the spitting and cursing Juanita.

She struggles too, but her resistance is less difficult to cope with and soon all three of them are sound asleep. I check their bonds, making certain they are secure so that if, by some miracle one of them should wake up, they cannot raise the alarm. Next I take the A3 signs, the tape, and my attaché case, now with the gun back inside it, with me as I leave the caravan and lock it securely.

I stick several strips of tape over the door and attach the A3 notices proclaiming that this vehicle is strictly out of bounds. Satisfied with my work at the caravan, I simply stroll back to the car park and drive Toby's car away. I park it several streets away and then walk back to school to go about my daily business, but only after informing the main office that I've had messages from Mr Marriott and Miss Cortez saying that they will not be in today.

'Oh, I wonder why?' says Bianca, one of the receptionists, with a saucy knowing wink.

'Yes, I wonder?'

At twelve o'clock I arrive at Lowbridge's office for an appointment I made earlier in the week. I have to move speedily or the whole scheme will fly out of the window. I have less than an hour before lunchtime, when the school will be heaving with pupils.

Lowbridge, of course, has kept her afternoon free in order to make certain she is available for any photo opportunity or interview.

I knock on the door and enter her office; as expected she is alone. Even though this is an official meeting my presence in her room still provokes a sneer.

'We need to be very quick,' she says; 'with all these television people on site.'

Now I must act more convincingly than I ever have before.

'We have a real problem,' I begin. 'We've found something in the old gardener's caravan and I think you should see it.'

'What's been found?' she asks.

'There is a considerable amount of money and some rather compromising documents,' I say, laying the bait.

'Documents? What sort of documents?'

'That's what I think you should look at.

'Well can't you fetch them here?'

I hadn't counted on her lack of desire to get off her backside and walk to the caravan. If I can't get her to come with me then everything is lost.

'It will be lunchtime soon and I don't think we should move these things through a crowded school. I really think you need to take a look yourself. Mr Colletti is already down there waiting for us.'

'What's he got to do with it?'

'He found the documents and the money.'

'Oh very well,' she says and heaves herself up. 'Come on then, you'd better show me.'

It takes a few minutes to exit the school and head out across the playing field to the caravan. No one is using the field this afternoon, due to the preparations for the trebuchet firing after school. In the distance I can see people milling around the great mediaeval siege weapon.

Gino is outside the caravan when we arrive. He looks agitated and nervous, which is hardly surprising.

'Mr Pike, I glad you bring Miss Lowbridge. I so worried while I wait for you.'

'Thanks for staying here Gino,' I say as I take out the key and unlock the door. I pull off the tape and the notices and then go in. Lowbridge follows and then last of all, Gino.

'Well, where is it?' she demands, her impatience building with every second.

'In the bedroom,' I tell her, 'under the bed.'

She's sees the three occupants, lying on the bed, as soon as she enters the room and spins around to face me.

'What's the meaning..?' she stops, having noticed the pistol in my hand. 'Quickly Gino, tie up her hands and feet.'

With his hands shaking he complies with my instruction and all the while he is doing it she stands there, staring defiantly at me.

'You don't think for one moment you frighten me, do you, Pike?'

'That's hardly relevant,' I reply, 'as I'm not here to frighten you.'

'You know this will ruin you and you'll spend a good few years in prison.'

'We'll see,' I reply as I check to see Gino has done his work well. 'Now put her on the bed with the others.'

Gino stands motionless, his eyes pleading with me.

'Mr Pike, perhaps we go too far,' he whimpers. 'Maybe we stop now. What she did to Shirley was bad, but I can't go through with this.'

'It's too late Gino, we have to carry on,' I demand, but the look in his eyes tells me everything; his nerve has totally left him.

He moves towards me.

'Please Mr Pike, we must stop this now. Please give me the gun.'

He continues to move forward; it seems I've been deserted.

'I can't,' I tell him, 'move back!'

He doesn't listen to me and keeps edging closer. I shoot and he falls back, clutching his bloodied chest.

'You mad man! You've killed him!' shouts Lowbridge. 'Help! Help!'

She screams, but soon stops when she sees me cock the hammer on the gun again.

'One more sound and you'll be next,' I say, indicating the bloody body of the PE teacher on the floor.

A short time later four bodies lie side by side on the bed; all of them sleeping peacefully due to the effects of the chloroform. Their bonds have all been removed and they now wear the Erotica underwear, as provided by Monica. This was without doubt the most difficult task I have been required to do. Seeing Juanita and Val naked was a pleasure to my eyes, but I can't say the same for Marriott and Lowbridge. However, having them all dressed in the same saucy undergarments is an essential element of the plan.

All I can do now is go back to school and wait until four o'clock. The sleeping beauties will wake up in their own good time. I take one final look at Juanita and Val and muse for a few seconds on what might have been before leaving the caravan, this time unlocked, and head back to the main building.

CHAPTER 21

FLYING CARS AND FLYING COWS

"Power tends to corrupt, and absolute power corrupts absolutely. Great men are almost always bad men."
Lord Acton

I'm sitting in the library with the other three candidates waiting for the decision. It's been tough going as the interview has been spread over two days. According to Dorothy Biggar, they felt compelled to make the process as rigorous as possible so as not to make the same mistakes they made last time.

This time I was included on the list, which I suppose was only fitting considering the job I've done in getting the school back on the road after the Lowbridge debacle.

So now I sit and wait to see if I am to be the future of Laburnum School. As I do my mind drifts back to that strange day many months ago, the day I took revenge on the people that had bullied me, threatened me, used me and abused me.

I'd left the four of them in the caravan still under the influence of the anesthetic drug and gone back to my office. There I'd waited until school finished at three-thirty and the kids began streaming home for the weekend. On this particular Friday however, many decided to hang back and watch the spectacular events unfolding on the sizable playing field. By the time I got out there the camera crew was already filming a reporter talking to Derek Forrest and several of the children who had been involved in the impressive construction project. Other reporters representing the local press and one national newspaper were also in attendance.

I stood and watched the recording crew go about their business as Derek went about his: enthusiastically showing them his detailed drawings and plans. At the conclusion of the interview Mr Forrest saw me and came running over.

'The car, Bob, you said you'd provide the car for the attempt,' he spluttered. 'Have you got it?'

'Of course I've got it. Shall I get it now?'

'Oh thank God!' he sighed with ultimate relief. 'Yes we need to start loading it.'

I walked over to the staff car park and got into Val's shiny new Mini and then drove it around the back of the school to where the expectant Derek Forrest was waiting. As I pulled up next to him I could see he was looking quite shocked.

'It's brand new,' he said as I climbed out of the little car. 'It's brand bloody new.'

'Does that matter?' I asked, innocently.

'Bob, do you realise what is going to happen to this thing? Do you understand how much there will be left of it when we chuck it over four hundred mertres?'

'Not a lot, I would imagine,' I replied, 'but that doesn't concern me and it shouldn't concern you. This thing has been donated to the school with the express purpose of it being used in the record attempt.'

'What idiot would donate a brand new car?'

'This idiot,' I replied pointing at myself.

He eventually overcame his surprise and unease at the prospect of using and totally destroying the vehicle and drove it away to be loaded into the massive slingshot of the giant trebuchet.

I strolled over to join in the party atmosphere that was fast developing on the field near the school building. We had an excellent view of the mediaeval weapon. Here I met with Dorothy Biggar who was busy sucking up to the Lord Mayor and our local MP. I stayed and chatted and said all the things I'd planned before I moved on.

I walked through the crowds of people gathering to witness what could be a unique event in the annals of Laburnum High School. I passed tables of inedible cakes, provided by Deirdre Harridan, the cookery teacher and without doubt the most vicious member of staff at the school.

'Have a cake, Mr Pike,' she snapped at me as I tried to slide past the array of terrible tarts and putrid pastries on offer.

'I'd love to Deirdre,' I'd answered, but I was caught in the wicked spider's web and unable to hide. 'I'll have one of those delicious looking fruit cookies.'

'What fruit cookies? We only have plain ones,' she replied, glaring at me through eyes I have always thought betrayed a nearness to insanity.

'A plain one then,' I said quickly.

Hastily I took the large burnt biscuit, thanked her profusely and disappeared into the crowd. Having examined the cookie I found it to be home to only four dead flies.

A sudden tapping on my left shoulder caused me to turn around and come face to face with Dorothy, looking more than a little agitated.

'Where is she,' Dorothy had asked.

'Where's who,' I replied innocently.

'Katherine, the Headteacher? Where is she?'

I looked pensive for a moment and then began scanning the crowd for a possible sighting of her.

'I can't see her, but I would have thought she'd be here by now,' I said. 'They'll be firing the thing in a few minutes time.'

'I know,' replied the Chair of Governors, 'and the TV people want to interview her before and after they fire it, to get a reaction. 'I can't believe this.'

She was about to scuttle off, then seemed to have an inspirational thought shoot in to her head.

'You'll have to do it, Bob,' she said. 'You can talk to the TV and say Ms Lowbridge has been called away on urgent business.'

And so with five minutes to go before the firing of the great machine, I was hauled off to speak with Maggie Williamson, the TV presenter charged with reporting on the event for the BBC.

'Well you're obviously very proud of the work Mr Forrest and the children have put into this fantastic enterprise,' said Maggie, as we both stood close to the trebuchet and watched Derek and his team carrying two halves of a brush headed concrete cow to the Mini Cooper and then load each half into the front and rear of the vehicle.

'What are they doing now, Mr Pike?'

'Apparently, in order to comply with the rules laid down by the Guinness officials, the car must carry the equivalent weight of four people,' I stated, making certain I sounded as if I was a leading authority on the subject. 'Usually people use sandbags, but we thought one of our famous concrete cows would be more appropriate.'

'Yes, ha, ha,' said Maggie, with a typical TV presenter's false laugh, 'and according to the children this cow has been designed to represent the Headteacher, Mrs Lowbridge.'

'Well you might think that, but I couldn't possibly say…'

'No, I bet you couldn't, ha, ha.'

She finished, or "wrapped up" the interview and I went back to stand with Dorothy and the V.I.P.s now gathered in the prime position ready to watch the event. The last act in my little drama was fast approaching and up to now things had gone better than I could have expected.

At this point, a student came running up to us and handed Dorothy a note. She thanked the girl, who happily ran off to watch what was happening. I peered from the corner of my eye as the Chair of Governors quickly read the message and then furiously screwed up the paper. Next second I felt another of the little woman's impatient taps on my shoulder.

'Come with me, Bob, I have something to do,' she said and then scuttled of in the direction of Derek Forrest. I followed.

'I need to go and get the Headteacher,' said Dorothy to Derek as he was going through his exhaustive list of checks before he was ready to fire the machine. 'Can you delay the firing for a few minutes until we're back?'

'No problem,' he replied. 'We'll need a bit more time, anyway, to make certain everything is ready.'

Satisfied she would not miss the firing, Dorothy once more scuttled off with me in tow and this time headed off across the playing field to the old gardener's caravan.

'Where are going Dorothy?' I'd asked in all innocence.

'I sent a message to reception asking if they knew where Ms Lowbridge was and they sent back saying they'd had a message that she was going to Old Bill's caravan.'

'Really! Whatever for?'

'That's what I want to find out,' said the little woman as she marched determinedly towards the caravan parked close to the very edge of the school perimeter. 'She should be up there talking with our important guests.'

All was quiet on the outside as Dorothy walked straight up to the door and flung it open. The instant she did there was a loud moan from the rear of the van; we went in. Again there was a load moan.

'What on earth's that?' quizzed the little prim and proper Chair of Governors.

'It came from in there,' I said. She immediately marched passed me and through the door leading to the small bedroom.

The scream of utter horror she produced one second after entering the room will remain with me for the rest of my life.

'Mr Pike, in here!'

Gallantly I ran to the aid of my Chair of Governors to face whatever hideous situation had caused her such distress. Even though I knew what to expect the sight that greeted me still urged my lunch to pay a return visit to my mouth.

Lying on the bed in a mass of entwined limbs, four sweat-soaked erotically dressed bodies writhed unpleasantly together. The smell of alcohol in the room was overpowering and all four seemed to be drenched in the stuff. Several opened bottles of spirits and wine littered the shelf and small dressing table. My entry indicated it was time for me to do some effective ad-libbing.

'Val? Val? What are you doing here?'

The only answer I received was a bleary eyed slur and a slight giggle as she slipped beneath the twisting bulk of anther body.

'Ms Lowbridge what are you doing? I demand to know?' screamed Dorothy. 'This is disgusting.'

'He did it,' slurred the PVC clad Headteacher, pointing an unsteady finger in my general direction. 'He did this to me then the bastard shot that teacher, Mr Colletti.'

'You're drunk, woman,' replied Dorothy, ignoring the strange accusations levelled at me. 'Get up and get dressed. You disgust me.'

'Val, how could you do this to me? I loved you so much,' I almost pleaded and then began to weep; the effect was excellent, even though I say it myself.

To make things even worse, or better, depending which camp you were in, Juanita and Toby, in their drug filled state were becoming very uninhibited and aroused. Even as Dorothy was demanding that the Headteacher get up off the bed, they had begun to copulate. Eventually the whole tableau proved too much for the little Scottish woman's sensibilities and she stormed out, with me in hot pursuit.

'I want you to take charge, Bob,' said Dorothy, as we marched back towards the crowds gathered near to the trebuchet.

'Of this event? Of course Dorothy,' I said.

'Of the school,' she replied. 'I'm suspending Ms Lowbridge forthwith, pending a Governors' hearing.'

'Oh,' I replied. 'I see.'

A member of staff came running over to us, waving as he ran.

'Mr Forrest says he ready to fire the catapult now.'

'Thank you, Mr Colletti,' I said; the timing could not have been more perfect. I winked at him to reassure him that things were still going to plan and he nodded back to acknowledge, before turning and trotting back to his position.

'The woman must be mad,' said Dorothy, not even bothering to comment on the accusation concerning the murder of the PE teacher, once he'd moved away. 'She's absolutely stark, staring mad, and a pervert by the looks of it. It's appalling behaviour and right here on the school premises; appalling and then to try and blame you after she'd been discovered.'

She continued to chunter all the way back across the playing field until we were once more standing with the V.I.P.s. Over the loud speaker Derek Forrest was just talking to the crowd and thanking all the children, for their help and hard work in constructing the great wooden beast that was sitting patiently, waiting for the moment when its power would be released.

Moments later the announcement everyone was waiting for was made. The trebuchet was ready to be fired. One of The Guinness Book of Records verifiers took over on the loud speaker and began the countdown.

'Ten, nine, eight, seven,' he began, as I could still hear the small Scottish Chair of Governors by my side raging at the behaviour of the Headteacher. 'Six, five, four, three, two, one, fire!'

Derek Forrest and two of the student's, threw their weight against the great trigger lever of the mediaeval siege weapon. There followed a loud creaking of timber and a whooshing noise as the huge counterbalance weights plummeted to the ground, swinging the mighty arm to a height of over forty feet in the air, attached to which was the slingshot containing the Mini with its concrete passenger.

The mighty forces involved helped whip the automobile off the ammunition table and high into the sky and then, as efficiently as predicted by Forrest, the slingshot released its cargo and sent it sailing out across the playing field. The thought of that big brush-headed cow sitting behind the wheel of my wife's car flying many metres above the ground brought a satisfied smile to my face.

The crowds of onlookers gave a loud cheer as they saw the great machine fling the Mini far into the distance. Then they watched in amazement as the car flew much further than expected; much further and a fair bit off the straight trajectory predicted. Perhaps the position of the cow in the car had cause an imbalance.

The theory was that the car would reach a distance of somewhere around about four-hundred metres. No one could have believed that this distance would be exceeded by over two-hundred metres. Nor could they have reckoned on the deflection of another thirty metres. It was, without doubt, a phenomenal throw and one hardly likely to be bettered in the years to come. However, this fantastic achievement was marred by one slight problem: as it landed, the Mini Cooper, laden with a quarter of a ton of concrete, ploughed into the old gardener's caravan, totally destroying it.

'Wow, I hope there was no one in that thing,' said the more than impressed Lord Mayor, as Dorothy and I simply stared at each other.

In the following days the facts about the death of four people in a demolished caravan came to light. People, especially staff at the school, were hardly surprised that the remains of Toby Marriott and his Spanish lover were discovered in the debris of the accident. Neither, apparently, were they surprised that my wife was also counted among the victims, as her affair with Toby Marriott, it transpired, was common knowledge.

What did cause a good deal of puzzlement was the inclusion of Ms Lowbridge in the "love nest." The reasons behind her involvement soon became the focus of staffroom speculation. However, one or two well informed sage's on the staff did allude to several meetings Ms Lowbridge had been having with Juanita Cortez leading up to the tragic day. Perhaps, some said, the feisty little Spanish lady had seduced someone other than Toby Marriott. This is where conjecture and reality collided dramatically as, in the course of their investigations into the tragic events of that fateful Friday, the police discovered several passionate handwritten letters sent from the deceased Headteacher to Juanita amongst her belongings. Apparently Lowbridge had become as enraptured by the sultry Spanish beauty as I had. What a strange and mysterious world we live in.

Juanita, bless her heart, was destined to become labelled as the villain in the whole sorry affair. She was blamed with luring poor, gullible Toby, the infatuated Lowbridge and dear naive Valerie into a doomed drunken orgy in the old caravan.

Poor, poor, sweet Valerie; what more can I say? I wanted to teach her a lesson; show her what it was like to be humiliated and then show her what had become of her precious little car. Unfortunately she was reunited with her stolen car in a violent and ultimately manner, which proved to be fatal. Poor Val; I will miss her dearly and when I see the roses growing in our garden I will always think of her.

For my part, as you can imagine, having so many traumas heaped upon me in one savage serving, I was rewarded with a massive amount of sympathy from everyone connected with the school and soon my office became the home for hundreds of condolence cards and messages of goodwill.

The Governors handed the control of the school over to me and made me Acting Headteacher once more; a role I accepted with the greatest humility.

Only one slightly loose end remained and that was Gino Colletti.

The PE teacher had played his part incredibly effectively, especially in the way he had "died" with a blank shot from the starting pistol; his theatrical experience was paramount in convincing Lowbridge I had totally lost my marbles. However, after the tragic accident happened Gino began to get very nervous, even blaming himself for the death of the four people. I needed to spend a good deal of time with him making certain he did not decide to let his conscience get the better of him. In order to ensure he is never able to "spill the beans" and spoil what has turned out to be a very profitable endeavour; I may one day be required to take drastic steps, but for the time being, I am satisfied with his loyalty.

I had set out to humiliate Lowbridge and have her leave the school in shame and disgrace and in that respect my scheme worked perfectly. She certainly was shamed and disgraced and, if she had survived, would have felt the Governors' wrath. What I didn't envisage was that she would leave the school in several heavy-duty plastic bags.

The destruction of the caravan left very little reliable forensic evidence and Dorothy's statement proved invaluable in providing key information. My involvement was less useful as, for many days, I was left traumatised by the loss of my wife and the discovery of her infidelity.

All this is in the past now and even Derek Forrest has made a near complete recovery from the breakdown he suffered in the wake of the tragedy. Still, he can rest assured that his name will remain in The Guinness Book of Records for years to come; not only as the builder and designer of the world's greatest trebuchet, but also as the name linked to the record number of people killed by a mediaeval siege weapon since 1807.

So now I sit with the other hopefuls waiting for the announcement as to who will be the next permanent Headteacher. Almost on cue the door to the Library swings open and Dorothy Biggar walks in together with Ted Barnacle, the Local Authority representative on the interview panel.

'Mr Pike, would you come with me please,' says the little Scottish woman, in as formal a tone as possible.

I follow; my heart is racing like an express train as she leads me in to a nearby office and asks me to sit down.

'Bob,' here it comes, 'the Governors have decided to offer you the post of Headteacher.'

I've done it! I have the Headship. Now the fun can really begin.

New year… New school… New job…

NEW BLOOD

by Chris F Coley

ISBN: 978-1-907219-12-2

Bob Pike is now the undisputed Headteacher of Laburnum High School and with his newly acquired authority he sets about stamping his own peculiar brand of leadership and management on the establishment.

When a new member of the teaching staff, the beautiful Miss Windmill, arrives at the start of the new academic year; Pike becomes so smitten by her beauty he uses his power and position to seduce the young woman.

Previous books by Chris F Coley

Amber Wolfe and the Shifters
&
The Daisy Chain
(a possible sequel to A Christmas Carol)

and coming next year
'No Retreat, A Story of Loyalty, Courage and
Dunkirk'
ISBN: 978-1-907219-05-4

This is the story of Wallace Moxon who was killed defending
the beaches of Dunkirk from the advancing German armies. His
son, the author's father-in-law, had kept a notebook in which
Lance Corporal Moxon had recorded the final orders he was to
carry out in leading a squad of young soldiers.

During the defence of Dunkirk Lance Corporal Wallace and his
men were allocated a position and given orders not to fall back
under any circumstance. In other words they were sentenced to
death or capture; the most the rearguard could hope to do was
delay the progress of the German troops.

The story of Wallace and the men of his final command is only
one of literally thousands of tales of tragedy that befell the
soldiers of the British army during those days in 1940; and yet
great solace could be taken from the very acts of gallantry and
bravery that made possible the whole endeavour of saving the
much needed fighting men and averting a total disaster.

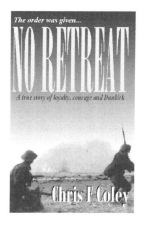

peakpublish

New Titles From Peak Platform

Peakpublish - Non-fiction

India Calls
by
Sudhindra Mokhasi
True Call Centre Stories

Playing for England
by
John Hemmingham
The England Supporters Band

Just Call Me Daisy
by
Lyndsey Bradley
Breast-feeding Mothers' Stories

Coal Dust to Stardust
by Jackie Toaduff
Billy Elliot Pales in
Comparison

The Best of France
by
Trevor Snow
8 Self-drive Tours

Jumping Fish - Fiction

Boji the Dolphin
by
Robert Alan-Havers
In Search of Independence

Not Quite Suicidal
by
Zoe Speakman
Life Can Only Get better

344 A story of the
Pretoria Pit Disaster
by
Andrea Jane Finney
Inspired by a Mother's Tale

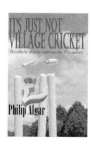

It's Just Not Village Cricket
by
Philip Algar

Selected Short Stories by
Bolwar Mahamad Kunhi
Translated work by award-winning
Indian Writer

Visit Peakplatform.com for more information